The warehouse looked deserted. Cobwebs covered the windows, and weeds grew up around the sides of the building. All the windows had bars on them.

Dennis Fielding followed Frank around to the back. Frank tried the knob on the door. To his relief, it turned easily. He opened the heavy door and stepped inside, with Dennis close behind.

The first person they saw was Nick Marino. Nearby, with their hands tied behind their backs, were Fenton, Joe, and another man Frank didn't recognize.

Marino lunged toward Frank, who sidestepped him neatly. Marino fell onto a large empty crate, overturning it. A kerosene lamp, which had been resting on the crate, fell over onto a stack of old newspapers. In seconds, a wall of fire blazed up, cutting them all off from the exit door.

They were trapped in a raging inferno!

The Hardy Boys Mystery Stories

#59 Night of the Werewolf
#60 Mystery of the Samurai Sword
#61 The Pentagon Spy
#62 The Apeman's Secret
#63 The Mummy Case
#64 Mystery of Smugglers Cove
#65 The Stone Idol
#66 The Vanishing Thieves
#67 The Outlaw's Silver
#68 Deadly Chase
#69 The Four-headed Dragon
#70 The Infinity Clue
#71 Track of the Zombie
#72 The Voodoo Plot
#73 The Billion Dollar Ransom
#74 Tic-Tac-Terror
#75 Trapped at Sea
#76 Game Plan for Disaster
#77 The Crimson Flame
#78 Cave-in!
#79 Sky Sabotage
#80 The Roaring River Mystery
#81 The Demon's Den
#82 The Blackwing Puzzle
#83 The Swamp Monster
#84 Revenge of the Desert Phantom
#85 The Skyfire Puzzle
#86 The Mystery of the Silver Star
#87 Program for Destruction
#88 Tricky Business
#89 The Sky Blue Frame
#90 Danger on the Diamond
#91 Shield of Fear

Available from MINSTREL Books

91

The HARDY BOYS®

SHIELD OF FEAR

FRANKLIN W. DIXON

A MINSTREL® BOOK

PUBLISHED BY POCKET BOOKS

New York   London   Toronto   Sydney   Tokyo

A MINSTREL PAPERBACK *ORIGINAL*

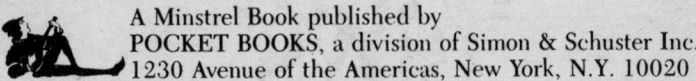 A Minstrel Book published by
POCKET BOOKS, a division of Simon & Schuster Inc.
1230 Avenue of the Americas, New York, N.Y. 10020

Copyright © 1988 by Simon & Schuster Inc.
Cover artwork copyright © 1988 by Paul Bachem
Produced by Mega-Books of New York, Inc.

ISBN: 0-671-66308-9

First Minstrel Books printing July, 1988

10 9 8 7 6 5 4 3 2 1

Contents

1. Over the Edge   1
2. Spotting Trouble   14
3. Flying Punches   25
4. The First Warning   32
5. In Deep Water   45
6. Larry Crawford's Story   55
7. Trapped in Toyland   66
8. Blowout!   75
9. Wild Shots   87
10. Where Is Fenton Hardy?   99
11. Clues and a Confession   105
12. To Atlantic City   116
13. A Witness Sings   124
14. Stakeout   136
15. Search and Seizure   146

1 Over the Edge

"Step on it, Frank," Joe Hardy said as his brother carefully maneuvered their dark blue van around a slower car. "Dad wants us to meet him in Philadelphia as soon as possible."

"Getting a speeding ticket or into a traffic accident won't help us get there any quicker," Frank said. "Relax. I've got a funny feeling we'll have all the action we want, and soon."

Frank shifted his sturdy six-foot-one-inch body in the driver's seat as he guided the van off the main highway and onto the exit for downtown Philadelphia. The wind blowing in from the window ruffled his brown hair.

Five minutes later, the van pulled up next to the Police Administration Building.

The brothers got out of the van and headed for the building entrance. As they stepped inside the building, Joe asked his brother,

"Are you sure Dad didn't say *anything* to you about this new case he's working on?"

Frank shook his head. "All he said was to get here as soon as possible."

"Well, it must be a pretty big case if he needs our help," commented Joe.

"All Dad's cases are big," Frank replied.

The Hardy brothers' father, Fenton, was a former New York City police officer who had become a well-known private investigator. Frank and Joe had worked on several cases with him, and they sometimes asked his advice when working on their own cases.

The brothers approached the reception desk in the lobby.

"This is where Dad said to meet him," Frank said, looking around. Joe was watching a group of young police officers in full dress uniform who were walking past them, laughing and talking loudly.

"Maybe *we* should think about becoming cops," Joe said. "Good pay, great uniforms, excitement, adventure—what do you say?"

"We already have a lot of excitement and adventure in our lives," Frank replied with a laugh. Then he added, "Let's think about getting through high school first, okay?"

Just then, Frank and Joe spotted their father walking toward them.

"I knew I could count on you two getting here today," Fenton Hardy said, smiling at his

sons. "Tomorrow would have been too late."
He approached the police officer behind the
reception desk and said, "The commissioner's
expecting us. I'm Fenton Hardy."

The officer looked at a list in front of him,
nodded abruptly, and said, "Right, Mr. Hardy,
you can go up."

"You're working for the Commissioner of
Police?" Joe asked his father as they headed
for a bank of elevators. The lobby was packed
with workers on their way out to lunch or
arriving to start their shifts.

"So, what's this case all about, anyway?" Joe
continued impatiently.

"Cool it, Joe," said Frank in a low voice.
"Dad probably doesn't want to talk about it out
here."

"Oh, right." Joe glanced around. "Sorry,
Dad."

They stepped up to the elevator door, and
Joe pushed the call button. When the elevator
arrived, they all quickly stepped inside.

Fenton turned to Joe and gave him an affec-
tionate smile. "I can understand how you feel,
Joe," he said. "But I think I'd better let
Commissioner Crawford do the talking."

When they got to their floor, a secretary
outside the commissioner's office recognized
Fenton and said, "You can go right in, Mr.
Hardy. Commissioner Crawford is expecting
you."

3

Fenton led the way through the door next to her desk into a large, richly furnished office. A tall man with silver-gray hair, broad shoulders, and bushy eyebrows, who looked to be in his early fifties, got up from behind a huge oak desk and stepped forward to greet them.

"Andrew, these are my sons, Frank and Joe," said Fenton Hardy. "Frank, Joe, this is Police Commissioner Andrew Crawford."

Frank and Joe shook hands with Commissioner Crawford. Even though the commissioner was wearing a well-cut three-piece suit, Frank thought he seemed like a Marine drill instructor. He looked gunmetal sharp, not a man to mess with.

Commissioner Crawford studied Frank and Joe for a moment.

He's sizing us up, thought Frank. But for what?

Finally, the commissioner gave a short nod and turned to Fenton Hardy. "I think they'll do. I think they'll do fine." He walked back to his desk and sat down behind it. Then he motioned to the three comfortable-looking guest chairs in front of the desk.

"I won't keep you boys in suspense," he said to Frank and Joe. "I've got two jobs. Your father is working on one. I need your help with the other."

"That's why we're here, sir," said Frank, knowing he was speaking for Joe as well.

4

"Before I tell you what I'd like you to do," continued Crawford, "your father and I will fill you in on his case."

"But because there's a grand jury investigation underway," Fenton said, "anything you hear in this room must be kept confidential."

"Definitely," said Joe.

Crawford smiled. "Good," he said. Then he leaned forward and took a deep breath. "Have you heard of a man by the name of Jack Brannigan?"

"He's some kind of crime boss, isn't he?" asked Frank.

"He's into a lot of rackets," Fenton said. "Protection, extortion, gambling. He has a habit of putting lots of muscle on innocent people."

"Brannigan's a notorious crime figure," Crawford went on. "He's very active in Atlantic City gambling operations, as well as in other, more illegal activities. He moved his operation to Philadelphia about two months ago. At that time, he also joined the board of directors of the Perelman Toy and Novelty Company. All perfectly legal—on the surface." His face was grim.

"The underworld grapevine is buzzing," Crawford continued. "It's rumored that Brannigan is up to something big. The district attorney has a grand jury sitting. They're looking into Brannigan and his activities, but I've

5

asked your father to investigate him, to find out what he's *really* up to in Philadelphia. We're sure it's illegal, but we need proof."

"You've nailed slimy crime bosses before, Dad," Joe said. "This should be a piece of cake for you."

"Thanks for the vote of confidence, Joe," replied Fenton, leaning back in his chair. "But this case has an extra, added problem."

"What's that?" Frank asked his father.

"Brannigan's attorney," responded Fenton. "Marcus Delaney is the sharpest criminal lawyer around. He's always been able to keep Brannigan out of jail."

"Brannigan and Delaney are a good team," said Crawford. "And a dangerous one."

"Sounds like you're going to have your hands full, Dad," Frank said.

Joe hunched forward in his chair and looked at the commissioner. "What's the second job? The one you need us for?"

"I was just getting to that," said Crawford. "While your father is busy tailing Brannigan and Delaney, I have something for you two that's very important to me. It concerns my grandson, Larry."

Crawford hesitated, a look of pain flashing across his face. The Hardys sat quietly and waited for the commissioner to continue.

"Larry's a cadet at our police academy," Crawford said. "The Crawfords have been on

6

the Philadelphia police force for generations. Larry is going to keep that tradition going, as I have and as his father did."

"What's the problem, sir?" Frank asked.

"Larry's getting in a lot of trouble at the academy, and I don't think it's his fault." Crawford's face darkened with anger. "I'm convinced that someone has it in for him. I need to find out who it is and why that person is trying to get Larry kicked out of the academy!"

Frank and Joe were silent. Police training is tough, thought Frank. Maybe Larry just couldn't cut it.

"I hate to say this, sir, but do you think the training is too hard for Larry?" Joe asked, as if he had read his brother's mind.

Crawford shook his head emphatically. "My grandson is a bright, capable young man. He can outshine any cadet there and should rank at the top of his class. He's got it in him to be *the* best," Crawford said proudly.

"What kind of trouble has he been in?" asked Joe.

"I've gotten reports that he's been failing tests, picking fights, and talking back to his instructors," replied Crawford. "If he gets only a few more demerits, he'll be expelled."

"Can't you ask his instructors about this?" Joe asked, relaxing back in his seat.

7

Crawford shook his head. "As police commissioner, I can't show any favoritism to my grandson. I don't think Larry would want me to, anyway."

"We can understand that," Frank said, nodding.

"People would say I was taking advantage of my authority," Crawford continued. "And maybe I would be." He stood up and slammed his fist on the desk. "But I *won't* let Larry continue to be victimized."

"How can *we* help?" Frank asked.

Crawford leaned across the desk. "I'd like you and Joe to enroll as cadets at the police academy," he said. "As cadets, you'll have the perfect opportunity to find out who has it in for Larry."

"Is it really that easy for us to get into the academy?" Frank asked. "I mean, wouldn't we have to apply first, then get accepted?"

Crawford shook his head. "I can arrange for both of you to become cadets, if you'll take on the job," he said.

Frank looked at his brother. "What do you think, Joe?"

"Do you have to ask?" replied Joe, grinning. "Let's go for it!"

"I agree," Frank said. He turned to the commissioner. "Commissioner Crawford, you just got yourself two new recruits."

Crawford's face broke into a smile. "Good,"

he said. He sounded relieved, as if a huge weight had been lifted from his shoulders.

Frank looked at his father, then back at the commissioner. "There's one thing I'd like to ask you two," he said.

"Shoot," said Crawford.

"You and Dad seem to know each other really well. What's the connection?"

Fenton explained. "Larry's father and I became good friends when we worked on a case together. He was a Philly cop, but an investigation led him to New York while I was still on the force. He was killed in the line of duty a few years later," Fenton said quietly. "Larry was only ten then. After I left the NYPD, I worked for the commissioner on some special cases."

Joe broke the brief silence that followed. "One more thing, sir," Joe said to the commissioner. "I'm seventeen and Frank's eighteen. Are we old enough to be cadets?"

Crawford pursed his lips and nodded. "That's a good point. You're supposed to be nineteen." He studied Frank, who was sitting calmly in his chair. "With your serious expression, Frank, I don't think you'll have any problem—you're almost that age anyway." Then he looked at blond, blue-eyed Joe. Joe returned the commissioner's gaze. "I suggest you try wearing a pair of windowpane glasses, Joe. That might help you look a little older."

"Will do," Joe said.

"You'll both be perfect for the job," Fenton said reassuringly. "And with luck, it'll only take you a week or two to solve the case. Then you'll both be back in Bayport, enjoying your vacation."

"Come on, Dad," said Frank, with a laugh. "This is better than a vacation, and you know it!"

"I should warn you," the commissioner said, a concerned expression on his face. "This won't be a fun case. Police training is hard work. And there's someone at the academy who knows how to make it even harder. Whoever's after Larry may try to make things tough for you, too. So be careful."

"Very careful," added Fenton. "At all times."

"When do we start?" Joe asked eagerly.

"The new term begins tomorrow," Crawford said. "Sorry to give you such short notice. But by next term, Larry could be expelled." He handed Frank a business card. "This has my private phone number on it. Feel free to call me any time you need to."

"We'll do our best for you," Frank told him.

"Then I don't know how I can thank you both enough," Crawford said. "I'll get to work arranging your enrollment at the academy and then contact you through your father."

Frank and Joe shook hands with the commissioner. Then they and their father left Crawford's office.

"I never thought I'd get to be a police cadet *that* fast!" Joe exclaimed once they were back out in the hall.

"And you don't even have to finish high school first," Frank said, throwing a grin at his brother.

Frank and Joe walked with their father to the building's parking lot, where Fenton had left his car.

Frank and his father were busy talking about the case; Joe walked ahead of them. Suddenly Joe stopped and stared at a very tall young man who had his hands on the hood of Fenton Hardy's car. When the man realized he'd been spotted, he quickly stepped away, got into the car next to Fenton's brown four-door sedan, and drove off.

"I don't like the looks of that guy," muttered Joe.

"What guy?" he heard Frank say behind him.

"There was a suspicious-looking guy hanging around Dad's car," Joe told him.

He hurried over to Fenton, who was tossing his sportcoat onto the front passenger seat of the car.

Joe told his father about the man he'd seen, adding, "Do you think he's involved with Brannigan?"

11

"It's possible," replied Fenton. "Would you recognize him if you saw him again, Joe?"

"Tall, thin, dark hair, high cheekbones," replied Joe promptly. "And he was wearing a thick gold pendant around his neck in the shape of a dollar sign."

"Well, I'll be on the lookout for him," Fenton promised. "Although, to tell you the truth, I'd be surprised if Brannigan has heard I'm investigating him. No one knows except Andrew and the D.A."

Fenton slid behind the wheel of his car. "I'm staying at a hotel in town, but I reserved a room for you two at a motel near the academy. It's the Liberty Bell Lodge."

Frank laughed. "You must have been pretty sure we'd take the case," he said.

"I was," replied Fenton, smiling. Then he added, "Since I know how to get to the motel, why don't you follow me there? You can check in, then we'll grab some lunch."

Frank and Joe sprinted off toward the front of the Police Administration Building and their van. As they got into the van, Fenton's car pulled up in front of them.

The city traffic was moving slowly but steadily. Joe was driving and had no trouble keeping their father's sedan in sight.

Soon they were on the interstate highway, accelerating to the speed limit. A metal guard rail ran alongside the shoulder of the highway.

Beyond the rail, an embankment sloped down to a deep ravine.

Suddenly Fenton's car swerved sharply to the right.

"What's going on?" Joe asked. "Dad never drives like that."

Before Frank could reply, Fenton's car careened into the passing lane, in front of a fast-moving tractor-trailer. The truck driver managed to brake just in time to avoid a crash. The blare of his horn split the air.

Fenton swerved to the right again, this time barely missing a collision with the brothers' van. Then he swerved back into the passing lane.

"He can't control the car!" Frank yelled, as his father swerved back to the right, coming dangerously close to the metal barrier at the edge of the ravine.

"We have to try to get him to slow down!" shouted Joe. He brought his foot down hard on the accelerator, and the van shot forward. When Fenton's car moved to the left again, Joe steered for the shoulder, hoping to wedge the van between his father and the railing.

He never made it. Before he could catch up to the sedan, it swerved sharply to the right again, directly in front of them.

Before the brothers' horrified eyes, their father's car tore through the metal barrier, plunging headlong down the ravine!

2 Spotting Trouble

"Dad!" yelled Joe, as his father's car tumbled down the embankment.

Joe screeched to a stop. He and Frank jumped out of the van and raced down the ravine.

Fenton Hardy's car lay on its side at the bottom, wheels spinning. There was a strong odor of burning rubber and spilled gasoline.

Frank and Joe ran frantically to the crash site. They saw Fenton, motionless, sprawled against the steering wheel. They hurried over to him.

Joe grabbed the door handle. "We have to get him out of here, Frank. The car might explode any second!"

Together they ripped open the car door, yanked off Fenton's seat belt, and quickly but gently pulled him free.

Just seconds after they had carried their

father safely away, the car exploded behind them. The boys instinctively crouched over their unconscious father, shielding him from the flaming debris that rained down from the sky.

When they turned back to look, they saw only a fiery heap where their father's car had stood.

Frank felt his father's wrist. "There's a pulse," he said, looking up at Joe. "But we've got to get him some help—fast!"

Joe nodded. "You stay with Dad," he said. "I'll call for an ambulance." He turned and started running toward the embankment.

"Call the police, too," Frank yelled after him.

Joe climbed quickly up the embankment to the van. Inside was a cellular phone, recently installed by the brothers' friend Phil Cohen. Joe made the two calls, keeping as calm as possible to avoid wasting precious seconds. Then he climbed back down the ravine to Frank and his father.

"He's still unconscious," Frank told his brother.

Joe looked up at the road. "What's taking those guys so long, anyway?" he asked.

"They'll get here in a minute. Go up to the highway and flag them down when they come. I'll stay here with Dad."

Each minute seemed like an hour, but soon

they heard the wail of sirens. Joe saw a police car and an ambulance racing down the highway. He flagged them down and led the two police officers and two paramedics with a stretcher and medical kit—who were half-running, half-sliding—down the embankment toward Frank and the unconscious Fenton.

The paramedics quickly checked Fenton's life signs. Then they carefully lifted him onto the stretcher and strapped him down.

"Is he going to be all right?" Joe asked anxiously.

"We won't know until we get him to the hospital," one of the paramedics said. "And from the looks of him, we'd better get a move on," he added grimly. He and his partner lifted the stretcher and started up the embankment, followed by the Hardy brothers and the police officers.

The officers asked Frank questions about the accident while Joe got in the ambulance with their father. As soon as the police finished their preliminary report, Frank jumped in the van and followed the ambulance to the hospital.

One hour later, Frank and Joe were pacing nervously in the waiting area outside the hospital's emergency room. Joe turned abruptly to his brother. "Dad's car was tampered with. And I have a pretty good idea who did it."

Frank nodded. "That guy you saw in the

parking lot," he said, adding, "Unfortunately, there's not much left of Dad's car to prove it."

They nearly jumped when a voice asked loudly, "Are Frank and Joe Hardy here?" A dark-haired intern was standing by the nurses' station, his eyes scanning the waiting area.

The brothers ran over to him. "That's us," Frank said. "How's our father?"

The intern smiled at Frank and Joe. "He's a very lucky man," he replied. "He's got a bad concussion and a couple of cracked ribs, as well as some contusions. I know that sounds serious, but it really could have been a lot worse, considering how bad that crash was."

"Can we see him?" Joe asked.

"He's regained consciousness, and his vital signs are good," the intern replied. "But he needs rest. You can see him in a couple of hours."

The brothers thanked him, and the intern hurried back into the emergency room.

"We'd better go back to the van and phone Mom," Frank said to Joe.

When they got to the hospital parking garage, where they'd left the van, Frank called their mother on the cellular phone and told her about the accident.

"An auto accident!" gasped Laura Hardy. "Is he all right?"

Frank told her about Fenton's injuries. "He's

going to be okay, Mom," he added reassuringly.

It took a lot of comforting and persuasion, but Frank finally convinced his mother not to come down to Philadelphia.

Frank hung up, thought for a minute, then picked up the phone and dialed another number.

"Who are you calling now?" Joe asked.

"The police. I want to get some info on Dad's car."

Frank spoke to the police. Then he called the mechanic at the service station where Fenton's car had been towed. He put down the phone and looked at his brother.

"Well?" demanded Joe.

"You were right," Frank said. "Someone did mess with Dad's car. There's not much left of it, but the mechanic thinks that the steering mechanism and brake pedal were tampered with."

"It had to be that guy I saw," Joe insisted. He pounded the top of the dashboard. "Just wait until I get my hands on him!"

"We have to find him first," Frank pointed out. "Then we have to find out if it was really him."

Joe shook his head. "I've got all the proof I need," he growled.

Frank squeezed his brother's arm. He was as

upset about their father as Joe, but he knew that his brother's temper, at this moment, wouldn't solve anything. "We have to stay calm and clearheaded about this," Frank said. "I wouldn't be surprised if Brannigan did send that guy to mess up Dad's car, but we need proof. And don't forget, we have our own case to work on."

"Why don't we see what Dad thinks about it?" suggested Joe. "He might want us to go after this guy."

"I doubt that," Frank said. "But we can ask him later."

The brothers checked a map of Philadelphia and drove to their motel. They checked in and quickly dropped off their bags and gear. Twenty minutes later they were back at the hospital.

They approached the nurse at the front desk and asked if they could see their father now. She nodded and gave them Fenton's room number.

When Frank and Joe stepped into Fenton's private room, their father was sitting up in bed. His head was bandaged, and his chest was wrapped with white hospital tape. Still, he greeted his sons with a smile.

"How do you feel, Dad?" Frank asked as he and Joe sat down in chairs next to the bed.

"Actually, I feel well enough to leave now,"

said Fenton. "But the doctor says I have to stay here for a few days, under observation."

Frank told his father what the mechanic had told him about the car.

Fenton nodded. "I'm not surprised. I've never known brakes *and* steering to fail at the same time by accident. And the car was inspected just last week. Someone *must* have tampered with it!"

"Dad, it was that guy I saw in the parking lot. I *know* it was," said Joe. "I think Frank and I should look for him."

"First things first," Fenton cautioned wearily. "I've got to get some rest. And tomorrow you enroll as police cadets."

"But—" Joe started.

"By the way, what about my car?" Fenton interrupted. "How bad is the damage?"

"Well . . . uh . . . Dad, I hope your insurance was paid up," Joe said.

"You'll have to rent a car while you're here," added Frank.

Fenton accepted the news with a shrug. Then he leaned back against the pillows and closed his eyes.

"If we could just find out who that guy is," Joe said, "I bet we could nail him."

Fenton opened his eyes and fixed them on Joe. "Look, I know how you feel, but I want you two to stay away from anything involving Brannigan. He's a crime boss with a reputation

20

for violence. If you do happen to come in contact with him or with Marcus Delaney, call Commissioner Crawford about it. But don't start working on *my* case. Got that?"

"Got it," Joe said reluctantly as his father gazed steadily at him.

"When you get a chance, call Commissioner Crawford and tell him what happened," Fenton said. "He may want you to look at some mug shots."

Then Fenton frowned a little, still looking closely at Joe.

"Maybe windowpane glasses *would* help," he said, breaking into a grin.

"Or maybe you could grow a beard," Frank suggested.

"Give me a break, you guys," protested Joe, running his hand over his smooth chin. "You want me to cover up this handsome face with glasses and a beard? No way!"

Frank and his father looked at each other and laughed.

"Besides, it's against cadet regulations to have a beard," Fenton said.

"And we couldn't wait the year it would take to grow," Frank said, suppressing a laugh.

"Okay, you two," Fenton said, laying his head back on the pillow. "I could use a little rest now. Keep me posted, and I'll call you when I get out of here."

Frank and Joe said goodbye to their father.

21

Then they left the hospital and drove back to their room at the Liberty Bell Lodge.

"First things first, like Dad said," Frank told Joe. "Let's order a pizza—then we call Commissioner Crawford!"

"Sounds good to me," replied Joe.

While the Hardys were waiting for their food to be delivered, Frank called the commissioner.

Crawford reacted to the news of the accident with shock and concern, but he was glad Fenton wasn't badly hurt. "I'm sorry to burden you with another problem at a time like this, but I have some bad news of my own," he told Frank. "Larry's in trouble again. He's been accused of cheating on a test. With these new demerits he's even closer to expulsion than he was before."

"Is everything set for us to begin tomorrow?" Frank asked.

"Yes, it's all been arranged," Crawford replied. "Check in at the Police Academy at eight-thirty tomorrow for orientation. Ask for Lieutenant Tom Redpath. He's chief of recruits."

"Will he know we'll be working undercover there?" Frank asked.

"No one at the academy knows," Crawford said. "I took the liberty of enrolling you as Frank and Joe Johnson. Too many people in the Philly police force know the name Hardy."

The commissioner continued, "Good luck, Frank, and be careful."

A few seconds after Frank hung up, the "full works" pizza and sodas arrived. While the brothers ate, Frank told Joe what Crawford had said.

"I wonder how tough the cadet training will be," Joe said.

"Yeah, me too," replied Frank between his second and third slice.

"Well, we're both in pretty good shape," Joe said. He studied his brother. "Actually, I might be in a little better shape than you are."

Frank almost choked on his fourth slice of pizza. "No way are you in better shape than I am," he said, giving Joe the once-over. "I've been working out all spring. All you did was play baseball—standing in right field waiting for all those fly balls that never made it out there!"

"How about a little bet?" Joe challenged. "Whoever scores lower, after however long we train, has to wash and wax the van until the end of the year."

"You're on!" Frank said, grinning. Then he became serious. "Do you really think someone's out to get Larry?" he asked.

"At first I thought the commissioner was being overprotective, but then I saw how much respect Dad has for him. . . ." Joe's voice trailed off.

"Yeah, I know what you mean," Frank's forehead wrinkled as he thought of something else. "But why would someone go to a lot of trouble to get Larry thrown out of the academy? Whatever the motive is, it must be big."

Joe nodded. "And what will happen if that someone finds out we're on this case?"

They both knew the answer to that. But it was Frank who put it into words. "Then we become the next targets," he said.

3 Flying Punches

The next morning, after breakfast in the motel coffee shop, the Hardy brothers drove to the Police Academy. Frank parked the van in a lot behind a long, one-story, L-shaped red brick building. Police cars used for driver training were parked in a driveway in front of the building.

Uniformed police officers entered the building along with young men and women in blue pants, short-sleeved blue shirts, and blue baseball caps bearing Philadelphia Police Department shield emblems.

The brothers found Lieutenant Redpath's office. There was a note taped to the door telling new recruits to report to the classroom across the hall. When Frank and Joe stepped into the classroom, they found it already filled with cadets sitting and chatting while waiting for the orientation to start.

25

Two of them were talking together in Spanish. Frank knew enough Spanish to understand most of what they were saying. Then one of them looked at Joe and said, "The blond kid must be visiting. He looks too young to be a cadet."

Frank whispered a translation to his brother, then added, "Maybe you should lower your voice an octave. At least you'll sound older."

Just then, a tall, barrel-chested officer in a crisp, clean blue uniform entered the room. He was a handsome, granite-faced man with close-cropped graying hair and a no-nonsense expression.

"I'm Lieutenant Redpath, in charge of new cadets. I'll be showing you around the building and grounds this morning. You'll get an idea of what we do here and what we'll expect of you." He looked directly at Joe. "Then you can decide if this kind of work is really for you."

Frank and Joe and the other cadets followed the lieutenant out of the classroom.

"We're very strict here, but we're also fair," Redpath explained as he began their tour. "If you follow instructions, obey the rules, and work hard, before you know it, you'll be part of Philadelphia's finest."

Redpath walked them up a long hall and let them look inside four classrooms. Cadets sat at desks in each room, listening to lectures.

"The recruits you see here began their training five weeks ago," Redpath said in a low voice.

"What are some of the things we'll be learning?" Joe asked Redpath as they continued down the hall.

"I was just about to get to that," Redpath said. He looked closely at Joe again. "We cover a lot of ground in the nineteen weeks of training. You'll learn about city ordinances, how to work with city agencies, how to fire police weapons, take fingerprints, perform first aid, drive police vehicles—"

"What about physical training?" Joe interrupted.

"There's physical training, all right." Redpath said this as if it were a challenge. "*Lots* of it. Not only for conditioning, but defensive tactics training. You'll learn pressure-point control, karate, judo, defensive holds, and blocking and kicking."

Frank and Joe looked at each other and smiled. They had used a lot of what Redpath called "defensive tactics" during their investigations. They felt sure the physical training at the Academy would be a snap.

"I'm curious," Redpath suddenly said to Joe. "How old *are* you, anyway?"

Joe gave the lieutenant his most innocent look. "I just turned nineteen, Lieutenant. I know I look young for my age. Everyone kids me about it."

"I can see why," commented Redpath dryly. To Joe and Frank's relief, he didn't press the issue. "We'll take a ten-minute break," Redpath told the group. "After the break, we'll meet at the front door. Then I'll show you the driver training course and pistol range." He left the new cadets and walked away toward his office.

Frank and Joe headed outside to get some fresh air, passing cadets who were on their way to other classes.

Just as Frank and Joe approached the front door, a tall, thin, brown-haired cadet with a sharp, pointed nose and a pale face pushed past them. He bumped against another cadet, nearly knocking him down, then yelled, "Hey! What are you pushing me for?"

"I didn't push you, Fielding," the other cadet insisted. He was about five-ten and muscular. He had a shock of red hair, large brown eyes, and a friendly freckled face.

"You *did* push me!" insisted Fielding. He jabbed the chest of the red-haired cadet with his forefinger. "You know, Crawford, I've had about enough of you." Fielding glared at the other cadet.

The Hardys exchanged glances. The red-haired cadet could be Larry Crawford, the commissioner's grandson.

"If you don't want to lose that finger, you'd

better remove it from my chest." Crawford slapped Fielding's hand away.

Joe started toward Crawford and Fielding, but Frank pulled him back. "We're here to investigate, not interfere," Frank reminded his brother in a hushed tone.

"Yeah, well, just stay out of my way," Fielding said to Crawford. Then he walked away.

The boys watched as Crawford shook his head and sighed. Then he headed down the hall, too.

"What was that all about?" Frank asked one of the older cadets who was standing next to him.

The cadet shrugged. "They used to be really good friends. But for some reason, they've been going at it a lot lately," he told Frank. "The redheaded guy is Larry Crawford, the Commissioner of Police's grandson. The other one's name is Dennis Fielding."

Before Frank and Joe could ask the cadet any more questions, Lieutenant Redpath approached them. When all the new cadets had gathered at the door, Redpath said, "Now we'll look in on a defensive tactics class."

Redpath led them to the gymnasium, where a blocking and kicking class was in session. The class was being supervised by Sergeant Hank O'Connor, a short, wiry man. Cadets in pairs were working in different parts of the room, practicing on each other. One cadet on a team would try to knock the other down while trying to block his or her partner's arm and leg moves.

When O'Connor saw Lieutenant Redpath, he stopped the practice. "I want you to work on your own for a while," he said to the class. Then he walked over to Redpath. The two men talked for a moment, then left the gym.

The cadets continued practicing. Frank scanned the room and saw that Dennis Fielding had been teamed with Larry Crawford. It seemed to him that Fielding was taking the training session a lot more seriously than his partner.

"Fielding isn't holding back his punches at all," Frank whispered to Joe. The Hardys moved down the sidelines to be closer to the action.

Suddenly Dennis slammed his fist into Larry's chest.

Larry staggered back, glaring angrily at his partner. "Hey, this is supposed to be a practice session, not a street fight!"

But Dennis just grinned at him. "Well, this is the way *I* like to practice!"

Fielding swung again, this time aiming a punch at Larry's face.

Larry took a blow to the cheek that snapped his head back. "Knock it off, Fielding!" he shouted.

"Good idea," Fielding replied with a laugh. He began a series of right jabs to Crawford's stomach, then let loose with a hard left. It hit Larry squarely on the jaw, sending him reeling back on his heels.

"This is getting out of hand," Joe said, frustrated as Frank held him back. "Why doesn't the sergeant or Redpath get back in here and stop it?"

Frank looked around the room. Neither Redpath nor the sergeant had returned.

"Why doesn't Larry fight back?" Joe said, his fist clenched.

The brothers watched as Larry Crawford blocked Dennis Fielding's jabs but didn't return the blows. He avoided the punches either by sidestepping them or by moving his head, right before they would land.

The other cadets stopped to watch the one-sided fight.

"C'mon, Larry, fight him!" yelled one cadet.

"Punch his lights out!" shouted another.

Larry dodged another punch to the chest, then dropped his guard for a moment. Fielding saw his opening. He plowed a hard left to Larry's ribcage. Larry doubled up, his head fully exposed to the other cadet's arsenal. Fielding flung a mean right. It caught Larry under the jaw in a brutal uppercut.

Larry staggered backward, then he hit the floor with a sickening thud.

4 The First Warning

Larry lay motionless on the floor. For a moment, Frank and Joe thought he had been knocked out. But then he blinked, groaned, and sat up slowly.

"Get up!" Dennis yelled.

"Fight him, Crawford!" shouted one of the cadets standing beside Joe and Frank.

"Don't let him get away with this," another cadet called out.

"What's the matter, chump?" sneered Fielding. "Can't make the grade for your hotshot granddad?"

Larry looked up at Fielding, his face red with anger. Then he got to his feet, eyes blazing. "Okay. You want a fight, let's fight!" He quickly threw a hard right that caught Dennis Fielding on the chin.

Fielding lurched backward. He recovered

32

and came at Larry again, moving in closer and aiming punches to Larry's stomach and face.

The two cadets threw punches at each other like prize-fighters in a championship bout.

"We have to stop this," Frank said. He looked at Joe and said, "Forget what I said before about not interfering."

"It's already forgotten," Joe said, eager for action. "You take Fielding. I'll grab Crawford."

Frank ran up behind Fielding and grabbed him around the waist. Joe reached for Larry's arms, pinning them behind the cadet in a full nelson.

"Let me go!" Fielding shouted at Frank.

"This is between Fielding and me!" Larry said, trying to squirm out of Joe's iron grip.

A few seconds later, Sergeant O'Connor and Lieutenant Redpath walked into the room. Frank and Joe immediately let go of Fielding and Crawford.

Sergeant O'Connor ran over to them. "The lieutenant and I heard some shouting. You two mix it up while I was gone?" he said to Larry and Dennis Fielding.

"They were just taking the class a little too seriously," Frank spoke up, hoping to save Larry from more demerits. "No harm done."

The sergeant looked at Frank and frowned. "You one of the new cadets?"

"Yes, sir," Frank replied.

33

"Don't sir me," O'Connor snapped. "I'm a sergeant. And you'll be doing yourself a favor if you don't volunteer opinions around here."

"Yes, sergeant," Frank said.

O'Connor turned to Larry. The cadet's face was bruised and swollen. "No harm done? From the looks of you, Crawford, you haven't learned too much about blocking and kicking."

Larry looked at Fielding. "Fielding started —uh—to show me a new move, Sergeant O'Connor, and—like the rookie told you—we just got a little carried away."

"That true?" O'Connor asked Fielding.

Fielding shrugged. "If you ask me, *he's* the one who got carried away."

O'Connor looked at Crawford again, then at the other cadets. "Okay, cadets, continue practicing. Crawford, Fielding, you two hit the showers." Then he walked over to Redpath and talked to him. Frank and Joe couldn't hear what he was saying, but they saw him gesture angrily at Larry Crawford, who was on his way to the locker room. Lieutenant Redpath stood quietly, his hands on his hips, listening. Finally, he, too, looked at Crawford, who was just exiting the gym, and frowned.

"Is it my imagination," Frank whispered to Joe, "or is O'Connor taking Fielding's side?"

"It looks that way to me, too," Joe said.

Finally Redpath shook his head, said something to O'Connor, then walked up to the new recruits. From the expression on Redpath's face, Frank had the feeling that he had filed away the report on Larry for future reference.

Redpath led the recruits out of the building to the driver training course. Then he took them on an introductory tour of the pistol range, housed in a low building a short distance away from the main building.

When they returned to the main building and Redpath's office, the lieutenant addressed the group: "Be here tomorrow at eight hundred hours. You'll get a haircut, fill out forms, be measured for cadet uniforms, and, after the swearing-in ceremony, you'll start classes at the academy. And those of you with mustaches or beards, say goodbye to them tonight."

He dismissed the others but asked Frank and Joe to stay behind.

He looked at his clipboard. "You two must know somebody," he said, frowning. "I won't ask who, but cadets don't usually join the academy before I interview them. And background checks have come through on you faster than usual. I don't know who's pulling the strings for you two, but don't expect any favoritism from me or the other instructors." He paused, then continued, "You're both in, if you still want to be."

"We still want to be cadets," Frank replied quietly but firmly.

"I'll be straight with you," Redpath said in a

steely tone. "I've never had much luck with cadets who get into the academy on pull. So I'll just tell you now—it may have been easy *getting* in. *Staying* in won't be."

The Hardy brothers nodded.

"That's all," Redpath said, dismissing them.

As they walked back to their van, Joe looked at his brother and laughed. "I can't believe it!" he said. "We haven't even been sworn in yet, and we already have a lieutenant and a sergeant warning us to watch out!"

Frank shook his head, opening the driver's door on the van. "I'm not laughing," he said, as he sat down behind the wheel. "O'Connor saw how messed up Larry's face was. I got the impression that O'Connor—and Redpath— just assumed it was Larry's fault."

"Well, with his record, do you blame them?" Joe pointed out.

Frank started the van and drove out of the parking lot. "Larry's record is a real problem," he admitted. "If someone is setting him up, he's been doing it for five weeks." He thought for a minute. "I guess O'Connor and Redpath —and the other instructors—just accept it when Larry gets into trouble."

"Do you think that the someone doing the setting up is Dennis Fielding?" asked Joe.

"We've only seen them together twice. And both times it seemed like Dennis started something. So Fielding is our number-one suspect," responded Frank. "At least for now."

"Let's just hope we can nail him before Larry gets expelled," Joe said. "And speaking of nailing people," he added, "I think I should check out some mug shots this afternoon. Maybe I can identify that creep who almost got Dad killed."

Frank's stomach growled. "That's a good idea, but can it wait until after we get some lunch? I'm starving!"

They stopped at a roadside diner and devoured bacon cheeseburgers. Then they drove downtown to the Police Administration Building. Joe used the van's phone to call the commissioner's office and arrange to look at mug shots.

When they arrived several minutes later, a sergeant ushered them into a room lined with stacks of books containing thousands of mug shots.

Joe sat down at an empty desk and began to leaf through the books. Frank sat nearby reading the Police Academy orientation booklet that Redpath had handed out to each new cadet.

After about two hours of staring at mug shots, Joe pushed the last book away, although he was only halfway through it, and looked up at his brother. "This is a total waste of time," he said, shaking his head. "I can't even *see* straight anymore!"

"Just a few more pages," urged Frank, now reading the sports page of the daily newspaper. "Then we'll call it quits."

"What do you mean, 'we'?" said Joe. But he retrieved the book and continued his search.

Suddenly Joe stopped turning pages and tapped a mug shot. "Frank!" he exclaimed. "I think I've found him!"

Frank jumped up and rushed over. He leaned over Joe's shoulder and peered at the photo his brother was pointing to.

"I almost missed him when I first saw it. His hair's a lot longer in this picture, but that's definitely his face. And he's wearing the same gold pendant, too." He tapped the picture again. "That's our guy."

Joe told the sergeant who had been sitting nearby that they had found the man they were looking for. Using one of the computer terminals, the sergeant called up the information on the man in the photograph.

"His name's Nick Marino," the sergeant read. "Age: twenty-seven. Hair: black. Eyes: dark brown. Height: six feet, five inches. Weight: one hundred seventy pounds. Two arrests, no convictions. Brought in twice, for grand theft at a jewelry store and stolen auto. Released on insufficient evidence."

"Nice guy," Frank said.

"Do you have an address?" Joe asked the sergeant.

She shook her head. "All it says here is that he was working as a used-car salesman at Classic Motors on Route One near the airport when the mug shots were taken six months ago."

"Let's check him out," suggested Joe.

The brothers thanked the sergeant for her help. A few minutes later, they were driving north on Route One. Classic Motors wasn't difficult to spot. It had a huge, flashing sign, and its parking lot and showroom took up an entire block. Frank parked the van in the lot of a diner across the road from the showroom.

They sat in the van and waited. Nearly half an hour passed without result. Finally they saw a tall, thin young man in sunglasses leave the showroom. He was wearing a white turtleneck sweater, jeans, and a glittering gold pendant.

"That's him," said Joe. "That's Nick Marino."

The brothers watched as Marino unlocked the door of a black late-model Italian sports car and got in.

"Some set of wheels. He must be an incredibly good salesman to sell enough cars to pay for that beauty," Frank said.

"What are you waiting for?" cried Joe. "Let's go after him!"

Nick Marino burned rubber leaving the car

lot, but before he was half a block away, Frank had caught up to him at the next traffic light.

"Don't get too close," Joe warned. "But don't lose him."

Frank shot an impatient look at his brother. *"You* want to drive?"

They followed Marino for about ten minutes through heavy traffic. Then he pulled up in front of a toy store. He jumped out of his sports car and went inside.

A few minutes later, Marino came out of the store carrying a square-shaped box, neatly gift wrapped. Marino got back in his car and drove off. Frank followed.

"From the way he's weaving in and out of traffic, I think he knows we're tailing him," Frank said after a few minutes. "He's definitely trying to lose us."

The next time Marino changed lanes, Frank swerved the van into the same lane behind him, narrowly missing a station wagon. The wagon's driver hit his horn angrily.

Marino and the Hardys continued a zigzag course, dodging cars and trucks as they wove in and out of the two lanes.

"We've hit green lights for almost two miles," Joe said breathlessly. "When is our luck going to change?"

"Right now," answered Frank, screeching to a halt at a red light.

Marino zoomed through the light, made a sharp left, and disappeared down the road.

"Only one thing left to do now," Joe said dejectedly. "Check out that toy store."

They cruised back to the toy store, parked in a nearby lot, and went inside. A little bell rang over the door when they entered. The store was well stocked with games, toys, and stuffed animals. Model airplanes hung from the ceiling. Shiny glass cases displayed finished car and ship models. Tables with model trains and a model race car setup filled half the room.

A short, rosy-cheeked, gray-haired woman stood behind the counter. She reminded Joe of his kindergarten teacher. The woman smiled at them as they approached the counter.

"And what can I do for you boys?" she asked cheerfully.

"I thought I saw my uncle come out of the store a little while ago," Frank told her. "My brother and I want to buy a birthday present for our niece. But we don't want to get the same thing he did. Do you mind telling us what it was he bought?" He gave her a description of his "uncle."

The woman's smile disappeared. She looked at the boys with a puzzled expression and then smiled again. "I'm sorry, boys, but I have a terrible memory for faces," she replied. "I'm afraid I don't know who you're talking about."

41

Just then, the little bell rang again. The door opened, and a tall, distinguished-looking man stepped into the store. He was wearing a well-tailored suit and dark sunglasses, and he looked to be in his early sixties.

The man walked over to a glass case along one wall and studied the display of model cars. The saleswoman glanced at him, fussed with the ruffles on her blouse, and said nothing for a few long seconds.

When she turned back to Frank and Joe, her expression was cold and completely business-like. "Well, how can I help you? What would you like to buy?" she asked impatiently.

"We'll have to think about it some more," Frank said, smiling. "Thanks for your help."

Frank and Joe left the store. When they got outside, they glanced through the window and saw the man approach the saleswoman. His face was grim as he spoke to her. The woman shook her head meekly from side to side.

"He looks upset about something," commented Joe.

Frank nodded. "And she looks scared," he added. *"Really* scared."

The brothers walked back to their van.

"I have a feeling those two know each other," Frank said, as he got back behind the wheel of the van. "I don't think that guy was just a customer."

"Neither was Marino," Joe said. "Whatever he got there, I don't think it was a toy."

"The question is," said Frank, "whether or not Marino and those two in the store are connected."

Frank steered the van back in the direction of their motel.

"We should tell Dad about Marino and the toy store. It might help him with his case."

"Too bad he can't help us with *our* case," Joe said. "If we don't come up with something fast, Larry Crawford's going to be an ex-cadet really soon."

A little while later, Frank pulled the van into a space in front of their motel room.

"I saw a deli up the block on our way in," Joe said. "Why don't I run over there and get some corned beef sandwiches?"

"Great! Get some hot peppers and dill pickles and sodas, too."

Joe turned and jogged off toward the deli.

The sun was just setting, and the weakening light cast heavy shadows on the trees and bushes around him. The neighborhood consisted mostly of private homes, many of them hidden behind tall hedges. The streets were deserted, and traffic on the road was very light.

On his way back from the deli, Joe thought he heard footsteps behind him. He stopped and listened, but there was only silence. He started walking faster and heard the footsteps coming closer.

Joe switched the brown paper bag he was carrying to his left arm. Now his right fist was free if he needed to use it.

The pursuing footsteps sped up, but just as Joe was about to confront whoever was behind him, he felt something hard crashing down on the back of his head.

Then everything went black.

5 In Deep Water

Joe lay motionless on the deserted sidewalk for what could have been minutes or hours. Slowly he came to.

"Ohh, my head," he groaned as he sat up carefully. He closed his eyes and breathed deeply. When the throbbing pain eased a little, he stood up carefully, picked up the fallen bag of sandwiches, and headed back to the motel.

Frank, a towel wrapped around his waist, was just heading for the bathroom to take a shower when he heard his brother's knock. He opened the door and was shocked to see Joe's dazed expression. "Joe!" he exclaimed, reaching out to steady his brother. "What happened to you?"

Joe handed Frank the bag and sat down shakily on the edge of his bed. He put a hand to the back of his head, wincing with pain. "Someone knocked me out."

"Did you see who it was?"

Joe shook his head. "I never got the chance. It all happened too fast."

"Was anything taken? Your wallet?"

"I don't think so," Joe said slowly. He felt around in his pocket. "No, I still have everything."

"You know, it could have been Marino," Frank said. "First he tried to put Dad out of commission. Now he wants to warn us off."

Joe lay back on the bed. "Could be," he said. His head was beginning to clear. "He knew we were tailing him. If he's involved with Brannigan, he probably thinks we're working with Dad."

"But how did Brannigan find out about Dad's investigation? It was strictly hush-hush," Frank continued.

"You've got me," said Joe, closing his eyes.

"My shower can wait," said Frank. "I'm going to call Dad *now*."

Frank checked the number and phoned the hospital.

"Someone just knocked Joe out near our motel," Frank told his father. "We think it could have been the same guy who tampered with your car." He told Fenton about finding and tailing Nick Marino and then added their theories and questions about the Brannigan case.

"The three of us will just have to be super-careful from now on," Fenton told him. "I'm hoping to get out of here tomorrow. Good luck at the academy."

"See you tomorrow," Frank said.

Frank hung up the phone and looked at his brother. Joe was sitting up and rummaging through the bag of food. He was obviously feeling a lot better.

Frank told Joe what their father had said. "I think I'll take that shower now," he added, heading for the bathroom.

He had just stepped into the tub when he heard his brother call, "Hey, Frank, come out here!"

Frank grabbed his towel and bolted into the living room.

"What's wrong?" he asked as he looked around the room. Then he sighed with relief. Joe wasn't being attacked again. He was sitting on a chair munching on one of the sandwiches, watching TV.

"Look at the screen!" Joe said excitedly, pointing with his soda can.

"That's the older guy from the toy store!" Frank said, moving closer.

He hitched up the towel around his waist, sat down on one of the beds, and stared at the

47

screen. A reporter was interviewing two men in a wood-paneled office.

"It's a news segment about Jack Brannigan," Joe explained. "That's him on the left. The huge guy with the puffy face and bags under his eyes."

Brannigan had a mop of curly, graying hair and wore a bold plaid suit and checked tie.

"The guy from the toy store is his lawyer, Marcus Delaney," Joe added. "The reporter is interviewing them in Brannigan's office at the Perelman Toy and Novelty Company."

"My client, Jack Brannigan, is a law-abiding citizen." Delaney was speaking directly to the camera. "He's done nothing illegal. But the D.A. and the police commissioner are determined to ruin my client's good name, trying to pin something on him in this unfair grand jury investigation. Commissioner Crawford would be better off answering some questions himself, starting with his mismanagement of the police force."

"Would you care to elaborate on that charge?" asked the reporter.

Delaney seemed to back off. "Not at this time. Let me just say that *perhaps* Commissioner Crawford ought to be investigated. But as far as Mr. Brannigan is concerned, I want the public to know that he is not engaged in anything illegal. He has bought a legitimate business here in Philadelphia, a business that

48

promises to help the entire community. And he is involved in some important philanthropic work. I don't think anything more needs to be said."

The reporter turned to Brannigan. "Your collection of antique toys is world-famous," the reporter said. "We also hear that you collect games. Is that true?"

A big grin spread over Brannigan's beefy face. "I bet I've got the best collection of board games around. Toys and games are my life! I export games worldwide. . . ."

Delaney put a hand on his client's arm, and Brannigan immediately stopped talking. The reporter looked back at the camera and signed off. The interview was over.

Joe reached forward and turned off the TV.

"So what was Delaney doing in the toy store this afternoon just after Nick Marino left it?" Frank said.

"He looked like he was yelling at the sales-woman. Maybe for talking to us. And did you notice how Brannigan shut up like a clam when Delaney touched him? He doesn't seem to want anybody to talk much."

The phone rang, and Frank picked it up. It was Fenton calling to ask if they had watched the evening news.

Frank said they had. "How do you think the toy store figures in the case, Dad?"

"I'll have to check on that," said his father.

49

"In the meantime, I want you two to stay out of the Brannigan case. Commissioner Crawford's counting on you to help his grandson. Stick to the Police Academy problem and leave Brannigan, Delaney, and Nick Marino to me, okay?"

"Okay, Dad," Frank agreed reluctantly. "See you tomorrow."

Frank repeated to Joe what their father had told him. Joe rubbed the back of his head and said, "I just hope Nick Marino is going to let us keep our promise to Dad."

The next morning, Frank and Joe entered the auditorium at the Police Academy and joined the other new cadets seated there waiting to be sworn in by the commissioner. After an hour spent filling out forms and getting measured for cadet uniforms, Frank and Joe saw Commissioner Crawford enter the hall.

The commissioner glanced at them, then looked away. Frank and Joe were careful not to give any signs of knowing him.

Lieutenant Redpath blew a whistle and told the recruits to stand at attention and raise their right hands.

In a short ceremony, Commissioner Crawford swore the Hardys and the other recruits in as cadets in training to become Philadelphia police officers.

When the swearing-in was over, the new

50

cadets were herded out of the auditorium to get haircuts.

"There isn't much left to cut on me. My hair's already short," Joe said, hoping to persuade the barber to leave it as it was.

"Not short enough," said the barber as he raised his scissors.

After the barber had finished his work, the brothers stood next to each other in front of a mirror, comparing their new haircuts.

"Remember how bald that white terrier up the block looked after he got his hair cut this spring?" Joe asked. "That's how I feel—bald!"

"I think I'm glad we're in Philadelphia and not Bayport," Frank said. "Our friends would never believe what we look like."

Next they were issued uniforms.

Looking at his cap, Joe said, "It's got the Philadelphia Police Department shield emblem on it." He read the words on the front of the cap. "'Honor, Service, Integrity.'" He put on the cap and turned to his brother. "Now I really feel like a cop!"

Frank put his hat on, and he and Joe looked in the mirror again. "Looking good," Frank said with an approving nod. "And if we keep them on, no one will ever know we don't have much hair left."

Frank and Joe spent the rest of the morning in a classroom, learning about state laws and regulations. It was an interesting class but a long one, and by the end of it Frank was fighting to stay awake in the hot, stuffy room.

At lunchtime, as Frank and Joe headed out of the building, they saw Larry Crawford in the hall. "He looks worried," Joe said to Frank. "Probably because of that cheating accusation."

Standing in line to buy hot dogs and soda from a lunch truck, the brothers saw Larry Crawford leave the building and head for the parking lot.

Moments later, they saw him behind the wheel of a bright red convertible, driving off the academy grounds.

A little while later, while eating their lunch, Frank and Joe spotted Dennis Fielding driving a rusty old white sedan. It backfired as though a firecracker had been shot off.

"Maybe they're just having a car war," Joe commented. "Fielding's probably jealous of Larry's convertible."

"Maybe he should talk to Marino about buying a new car," Frank replied with a laugh.

After lunch, Sergeant O'Connor ordered the cadets to report to the indoor swimming pool. "You'll take a swimming test," he told them. "But let me just warn you this test is no picnic. Be ready for a real workout!"

Both Frank and Joe passed the swim test easily. When it was over, they and the other recruits stood around the Olympic-size pool watching some of the cadets practice lifesaving maneuvers. Larry Crawford and Dennis Fielding were working on their dives at the diving pool.

Frank and Joe moved closer to the diving pool. They saw Larry do a jackknife into the pool. He surfaced, floated to the edge of the pool, and climbed out.

"He's a good diver," Joe observed. "Wonder what kind of swimmer he is."

"There's Dennis Fielding," Frank said. Fielding stood on the board, raised his arms slowly over his head, and made a clumsy plunge into the pool.

"That was a really lazy dive," commented Joe. "I hope I never have to be saved by *him*."

Moments later, the brothers saw Larry back on the diving board. Fielding was behind him on the steps, waiting his turn to dive.

"Nice form," Frank noted after watching Larry dive off the board.

Sergeant O'Connor glanced at Fielding. Then he turned his gaze on Larry, who was doing a strong crawl stroke across the pool. Larry did an underwater somersault turn against the end of the pool and swam toward the ladder just as Dennis Fielding dove into the water.

The brothers watched as Larry and Fielding practically collided in the middle of the pool.

Fielding shot out a hand and began splashing water in Larry's face. "Okay, so you get a score of ten for diving," Fielding taunted. "So what. Now let's see which of us can hold his breath underwater longer."

Before Larry could respond to the challenge, Dennis took a deep breath and pulled him underwater.

"What's Fielding up to now?" Joe said.

"I don't know, but I don't like it," Frank replied. "He didn't give Larry time to take a breath."

A minute later, they saw Dennis Fielding surface. He climbed out of the pool and looked around nervously. Then he headed quickly into the locker room.

"Frank," said Joe. "Larry's still down there!" Without hesitating, Frank dove into the pool. A moment later, he came to the surface with Larry in tow. Larry was gasping and sputtering. He looked as though he didn't even know where he was.

Larry grabbed at Frank in panic. Both of them sank under the water like stones.

Joe realized if he didn't do something fast, his brother and Larry would drown!

6 Larry Crawford's Story

Joe dove into the pool. Underwater, he saw Frank struggling to pull free and help Larry. Joe pulled Larry away from Frank and got him in a lifesaving hold across his chest. Frank rose to the surface, and together the brothers pulled Larry to the edge of the diving pool.

Some of the cadets from Larry's class came rushing over. Two of them helped Frank and Joe lift Larry out of the pool.

Larry doubled up and began to cough up some water. After a moment, he gasped, "I'm all right! Leave me alone!"

"What happened?" One of the cadets asked Larry.

"I guess I'm not as good a swimmer as I thought," Larry replied breathlessly. "I just panicked." With that, he slowly walked off toward the locker room.

Frank didn't buy Larry's explanation. He

glanced at his brother. Joe didn't look as though he bought it either.

The lifesaving class was over. The cadets headed for the locker room to shower and change. Frank and Joe saw Larry drop wearily onto a bench outside the locker room. He leaned back and closed his eyes.

"Larry's a good swimmer," said Joe. "But he didn't have much of a chance with Fielding pulling him under the water like that."

"What I don't understand is why Larry won't stand up to Fielding."

A few moments later, Larry came over to the brothers and introduced himself.

"Thanks for going in after me," Larry said abruptly.

"Anytime," Frank said casually. "By the way, I'm Frank Johnson, and this is my brother, Joe."

"We're new cadets here," Joe added.

"Yeah, I know," Larry said, nodding. "I remember you from the defensive tactics class yesterday." He frowned, and his voice grew colder. "Look, I appreciate what you did then and today, but from now on do me one more favor, huh? Let me handle things myself, okay?" The cadet turned sharply and walked away.

"I don't get him," Joe said when Larry was out of earshot. "We saved his life, and he acts like an iceberg."

Frank watched Larry go into the locker room. "I know what you mean," Frank said. He thought for a minute, then asked his brother, "Where was Sergeant O'Connor?"

"He was around the pool when Larry and Fielding started their dives," Joe replied. "But I didn't see him after that."

"O'Connor never seems to be around when Fielding goes after Larry," Frank said.

"And he even teams them up, knowing they don't get along," Joe added.

"Maybe he teams them up on purpose, so one or the other loses his temper," replied Frank. He looked at his brother. "You know, Larry does seem to have a pretty short fuse. No matter what his grandfather thinks, maybe he *has* taken on more than he can handle, and it's making him nervous."

"I don't know about that," Joe said, shaking his head. "He could just be worried about getting kicked out of the Academy."

"Maybe you're right," replied Frank. He glanced at the clock on the wall. "Come on, we'd better get dressed or we'll be late for our next class."

When they got to the locker room, the Hardys saw Larry and Fielding again. The room was empty except for the two cadets and a few of their classmates.

Larry was getting something out of his locker

when Fielding suddenly banged his shoulder against Larry's locker door.

"Hey, watch it!" Fielding shouted at Larry. He held his shoulder as if he were in pain. The other cadets, who were on their way out the door, turned to see what was going on.

It was hard for Frank and Joe to remember who landed the first punch after that. All they could see were fists flying.

"This is getting ridiculous," Frank said, slamming his towel down on the wooden bench.

"Here we go again," Joe said, rushing to help his brother.

They restrained Larry and Fielding. Just as the brothers got hold of the two cadets, they heard an angry voice shout, "Okay, what's going on here?"

The four of them looked toward the door and saw Sergeant O'Connor frowning at them. The cadets standing by the door left quickly.

"Let them go!" O'Connor shouted to Frank and Joe. "You rookies get your things and get out of here. This has nothing to do with you."

Frank and Joe dropped their holds on the two cadets and headed for their lockers.

"I'm getting pretty tired of this rivalry you have going, Crawford," they heard O'Connor say sternly. "I don't know what you have against Fielding, and I don't care. You're getting another demerit for this."

He glared at Larry. "I'll have to report this to Lieutenant Redpath," O'Connor continued. "You have a real attitude problem, Crawford. You better watch your step, or you'll be out on your ear." O'Connor turned and marched out of the locker room.

Frank glanced around the open door of his locker. He noticed a smug expression on Dennis Fielding's face as he followed the sergeant out of the room.

Larry shut his locker door. Then he, too, left the locker room.

Frank dug into his pants pocket for some change for a soda. Instead of the change, he pulled out a wrinkled piece of paper that had been tucked into his pants pocket. Frank read what was written on the crumpled-up note. Then he handed the note to his brother.

Joe took the note, read it, and gave a low whistle. "'Drop out of the Academy now or you'll be sorry!'" He looked at Frank. "Nice mail you're getting."

"Did you notice the handwriting?" Frank said. "It's practically illegible. It looks like whoever wrote that note decided to disguise his handwriting."

"Right," agreed Joe. "But who wrote it?"

"That," said Frank, "is what we have to find out."

After they finished their classes for the day,

Frank and Joe walked to their van. Joe got behind the wheel.

"What I want to know is how our writing friend stashed that note in my locker," Frank said thoughtfully. "The door was locked!"

"These are combination locks," replied Joe. "Someone either knew the combination or knew how to open this type of lock."

Frank shook his head and sighed. "With a building full of cops and cadets, it could have been anyone," he said. "And there's no way we can trace the handwriting on the note."

"Well, we can talk more about this case over my favorite brain food—pizza," Joe said. "Let's try that place near here—the Magic Pizza."

"Good idea. It's supposed to be a hangout for the cadets. Maybe we'll overhear something that will help us with this case."

The Magic Pizza was packed with cadets talking, laughing, and eating. While they waited in line for a table, Frank and Joe spotted Larry Crawford—dressed in stylish street clothes—sitting by himself in a booth. When he saw the Hardys, he motioned at them to come over.

He smiled at Frank and Joe and asked them to sit down. "I apologize for the way I acted back at the pool," he told them. "I'd like to treat you to dinner. It's my way of thanking you for what you did back there, and yesterday."

"We accept," Frank said, looking at a menu. "The apology *and* the pizza."

"It's really unfair," Joe said to Larry. "O'Connor seems to be blaming all your fights with Fielding on you."

"He doesn't seem to think Fielding is capable of messing up," Frank put in.

"Oh, you noticed that, too?" Larry said with a grim smile.

Just then, a gum-snapping waitress came over to take their order. Larry turned to Frank and Joe. "Is pizza with everything on it okay with you?" he asked.

The brothers nodded. Frank slapped the menu behind the salt and pepper shakers.

"One kitchen sink," said the waitress, writing the order down on her pad. She looked at them and shook her head. "You cadets must have stomachs like granite."

"We do," replied Joe, as his granite stomach rumbled in anticipation.

The waitress popped her chewing gum as she walked away.

Frank turned to Larry and said, "We saw Fielding pull you under the water. He didn't give you a chance to take a breath."

Larry's smile faded. "I know. And once we were in the water, I felt him push me down toward the bottom of the pool."

"Why haven't you told your superiors about Fielding?" asked Joe.

Larry's lips twisted. "I don't like the idea of running to O'Connor and Redpath every time Dennis does a number on me." He gave a huge sigh. "I have other reasons, too. Besides, I'm not sure they'd believe me anyway. Especially not O'Connor."

"Do you think Fielding wanted you to drown?" Frank asked.

Larry shook his head, then shrugged. "I doubt it. He doesn't hate me *that* much. At least, I don't think so. I think he just got a little carried away—again. He has problems, too."

"Why do you think he hates you at all?" Joe asked.

"I don't know," Larry said, avoiding Joe's eyes. "We were good friends all through high school, and afterward. I don't know what happened."

Frank looked at Larry. He was sure that Larry was hiding something. But what?

Larry continued, "Maybe he's jealous. My grandfather is police commissioner, if you didn't already know. Fielding seems to think that's giving me some kind of edge at the academy. If anything, being the commissioner's grandson has made it tougher for me. And what's worse, I get the feeling some of the instructors think the same way Fielding does about me."

"Sergeant O'Connor, for one," Joe said. "He takes Fielding's side every time."

"I don't know why O'Connor doesn't like me," Larry said, shaking his head. He paused for a moment. Then he said, "Look, I appreciate what you two did for me. But don't be there too often when I mess up, okay? O'Connor can be just as tough on you as he is on me. Besides, I like to stand on my own two feet—when people let me. Anyway," he added. "I'm under a lot of pressure right now."

"Maybe you're just trying a little too hard," suggested Frank.

"Maybe you're taking police training *too* seriously," Joe put in. "Putting pressure on yourself."

"You're both right," Larry said. "But there's a good reason why I'm overdoing it."

"We're listening," Frank said.

"The Crawfords have been cops for generations," Larry explained. "My dad was a cop. He died 'in the line of duty,' as they say."

"That's rough," Frank said sympathetically.

After a brief silence, Larry went on. "What it boils down to is"—he paused, as if he were thinking this for the first time—"it's just that I guess I don't want to be the one to break the family tradition. It means too much to my grandfather."

So being a cop doesn't mean that much to Larry, Frank thought to himself.

Finally the pizza arrived at their table, and conversation shifted to other topics, including their classes and what the Hardys thought of the instructors they'd had so far.

"Larry's a nice guy," Joe commented, as he and Frank drove back to the motel after dinner.

"I wish we could tell him what we're *really* doing at the academy," Frank said. "I don't think his only problem is that he's trying too hard."

Joe agreed. "Fielding is after him for sure," he said. "And I have a hunch O'Connor's setting him up, too."

Back at the motel, the brothers had a surprise visitor—their father. He had been released from the hospital, and, apart from a small bandage on his forehead near the hairline, he hardly looked like he'd just been in a serious car accident.

"I thought you'd want to know that Commissioner Crawford got a break in the Brannigan case," Fenton told his sons. "He received an anonymous phone call this morning from a man claiming to have evidence against Brannigan and some illegal activities he's involved in. The evidence is a ledger. Some of Brannigan's business transactions are recorded in it. It looks like the case is finally moving."

Fenton rubbed the patch on his forehead lightly. He noticed a half-eaten sandwich from the night before on the dresser. "Actually, I came over here to ask you out to dinner,"

Fenton said. He picked up the remains of the sandwich as if it were a dead bug and dropped it in the garbage. He sat down on the edge of Frank's bed, took out his handkerchief, and wiped a dab of mustard from his hand.

"How is *your* case going?" Fenton asked. "Any new leads?"

"We think we know at least one person who might be setting up Larry," Frank said.

"In fact, we had dinner with Larry," Joe added.

"Maybe you should try to have dinner with your suspect next," Fenton suggested with a grin.

The phone rang. Joe picked it up.

"Hello," he said. "Oh, hi, Commissioner. Yes, Dad's here. Hold on a minute."

Joe handed the phone to his father. Fenton listened for a few minutes, then frowned. "I'll be right over," he said. Then he hung up, looking angry and frustrated.

"What's wrong?" Frank asked.

Fenton looked at Frank and Joe. "Andrew's special investigators went to the meeting place to pick up the witness. But he was gone—and so was the ledger!"

7 Trapped in Toyland

After Fenton Hardy left, Frank tried to concentrate on his homework, but his mind was on the Brannigan case. He looked at Joe. His brother was lying on his bed, reading the newspaper.

"Aren't you going to study?" Frank asked.

Joe didn't answer him. He was too busy reading an article in the financial section.

Frank got up and glanced at what Joe was reading.

"I didn't know you read anything in the paper except the sports pages and the comics," Frank said.

"I happened to notice this on the front page of the financial section." Joe pointed to the article and said, "Some big toy and game manufacturer has been taken over."

"So what?" Frank asked. "Takeovers of big companies happen all the time."

"I don't know," Joe said, folding the paper back up. "Toys have kind of been on my mind ever since we visited that toy store and saw that interview with Brannigan. I guess that's why the article caught my attention."

A thunderous knock on their door made them jump.

"Who is it?" called Frank. Instead of an answer, there was another loud knock.

Frank moved to the door and opened it slowly, keeping it on the chain.

Frank's eyes widened with surprise when he saw that their visitor was Larry Crawford. He unlatched the chain and opened the door wide.

Larry stormed into the room. It was obvious he was furious about something. He whirled around to face Frank and Joe.

"I just got it out of my grandfather," Larry fumed. "He sent you guys to spy on me!"

Frank and Joe looked at each other.

"I should have known it!" he cried. "You're just a couple of snoops!"

"Didn't the commissioner tell you why we're at the academy?" Frank asked.

"It isn't what you think," Joe added. "Let us tell *our* side of the story."

"It's just like him," Larry said as if he hadn't heard Joe. "Planting you two as cadets to baby-sit me. Maybe that's part of the reason I mess up so much. He doesn't think I can tie my own shoes, much less stand on my own two feet. Maybe he's got me wondering about that myself, so I keep tripping up."

"Look, Larry, sit down and relax, okay? Let's talk this over," Frank said quietly.

It took a while, but Frank and Joe finally got Larry to calm down and listen to them. Frank sat down next to Larry on the bed; Joe sat in a chair in the corner of the room. Together, they told him why Commissioner Crawford had assigned them to the academy.

"We're not checking *you* out, or playing bodyguard," Frank finished.

"We're trying to find out who's setting you up," added Joe. "And right now, our prime suspect is Dennis Fielding."

"Our dad knew your father," Frank told Larry. "When they were both cops. Dad's working on a case for the commissioner. If your grandfather didn't tell you, our names aren't Johnson. We're Frank and Joe Hardy. We're the sons of Fenton Hardy, the detective.

"Maybe I shouldn't have told you that," Frank continued. "It's supposed to be top secret. But if you know the whole story, you can work with us."

Larry looked at the brothers. "That's okay," he said. "I know about your father already."

"What?" exclaimed Frank. "But how?"

"I overheard my grandfather on the phone

weeks ago talking with your father about investigating Jack Brannigan."

Larry scowled at the Hardys. "I don't like the idea of you guys shadowing me everywhere," he said. "It's as if he thinks I always need his help. Like I can't do anything for myself. He's kept tabs on me all my life."

"We won't crowd you," Frank promised. "But just let us do our job, okay?" He paused for a moment, then an important question crossed his mind. "Larry, did you tell anybody what you overheard—about Dad and the Brannigan case?"

Joe leaned forward in his seat, waiting for Larry's answer. There was a long pause.

"I told Dennis Fielding," Larry finally admitted.

Joe bolted from his chair. Frank stared at Larry. "You told *Fielding?*" Joe asked in disbelief.

Larry nodded. "It was just after we started at the academy. We were still friends then. I know it's hard to believe, but Dennis can be one of those guys you're positive you can trust."

"So Fielding must have tipped off Brannigan about Dad," Frank said thoughtfully.

"And Brannigan and Marino were just waiting for Dad to come to Philly so they could get rid of him," Joe added angrily.

"What are you talking about?" Larry asked, surprised at Joe's outburst. He ran a hand through his red hair and looked at Frank for an explanation.

Frank told him about their father's accident two days earlier.

"Look, guys, I'm really sorry," Larry said in a horrified voice. He turned to Joe, who was glaring at him. "Joe? Please believe me. I swear I didn't know anything like that was going to happen."

Joe relaxed a little. "Let's just forget about it, okay?" He looked at his brother. "Do you think Fielding is working for Brannigan?" he asked Frank.

"That's exactly what I think," said Frank. "And Larry's the fall guy. Remember what Delaney said during that interview? How he was going to look into mismanagement in the police department? He meant the academy."

"Right. Suppose the commissioner's grandson is suddenly exposed as a cheat. Then they can make allegations that the commissioner is trying to cover up for him. Maybe Delaney figures Crawford will get the D.A. to drop the grand jury investigation. The public will be crying for Crawford to clean his own house first."

"Right," agreed Frank.

Larry had been looking back and forth at

Frank and Joe, his mouth open. "You guys are *amazing!*" he said finally. "How did you get to be such good detectives?"

"Well, we *have* solved a few cases before," Joe said, trying to sound modest.

"But we haven't really solved this one yet," Frank continued. "We still need proof. But one thing's for sure—we're involved in the Brannigan case now, whether we like it or not!"

"I agree," said Joe. "So, now what do we do?"

"I want to go back to that toy store and do a little investigating," Frank said. He quickly told Larry about seeing Marino and Delaney at the store.

"Guess we'd better get moving," Joe said as he picked up the phone and dialed Fenton's hotel room. He let it ring for a while, then he hung up. "No answer. Dad must still be out with the commissioner." He looked at his brother. "We'll tell him when we get back," Frank said.

"Look, I'm involved in this case, too," Larry said. "I'm coming with you guys!"

The brothers tried to change Larry's mind, but he insisted on going along. Finally, they agreed and left the Liberty Bell Lodge with their new friend in tow.

It was eleven o'clock by the time they reached the store. Frank parked the van on a side street. The Hardys and Larry crept around the back of the store and heard voices coming from the rear of the building. They stood below a small rear window. Frank and Larry gave Joe a foothold and hoisted him up to the sill so he could look inside. Joe hung outside the window for a minute or two, surveying the scene. Then he let himself drop to the ground. Frank, Joe, and Larry talked in hushed tones.

"It's some kind of storeroom," Joe whispered. "Nick Marino is in there. So is the saleswoman we talked to. They're sitting at a card table, playing Monopoly, if you can believe that."

"It's after midnight," Frank said, puzzled. "What are they doing playing Monopoly at this hour?"

"They might be killing time," Joe suggested. "Waiting for someone."

"Or holding someone," Frank said. "The missing witness."

"Maybe," Joe said. "But I didn't see anyone else in the room."

"See if you can hear anything else," Larry said. He and Frank hoisted Joe up to the window again.

After a few minutes, some rock music started to seep out of the room. Joe dropped to the ground again.

"The woman said, 'Marc said getting to the

old man through the kid is really working,'"
Joe told them. "Then Marino said, 'If anything
goes wrong, we'll move everything to the museum.' That was all I could hear. They turned
on the radio after that."

Frank spotted another window farther back
in the building. He pointed to it.

"Two of us should try to get inside through
that window. One of us can stay here and stand
guard."

Larry agreed to be the lookout. "If I hear
anyone coming, I'll let out a whistle."

When they reached the other window,
Frank hoisted Joe up onto the ledge. Joe raised
the window and climbed inside. Larry gave
Frank a foothold up to Joe's extended arms,
and Joe pulled his brother up.

The room the brothers sneaked into was
pitch dark. Only the soft sound of the radio in
the other room broke the silence. Then Frank
heard another sound.

"Your shoes squeak!" he whispered to Joe.
"Better take them off."

Joe reached out in the dark to find a wall to
lean against while he took off his shoes. But
where he'd thought there was a wall was thin
air. Joe fell against a shelf. His right hand shot
out, and he tried to steady himself. He felt his
hand flick some kind of switch.

Suddenly a loud whirring sound shattered

73

the quiet. A mechanical voice boomed out, "Ho, ho, ho! I'm Santa the Robot! Ho, ho, ho!" Then the voice began to sing "Jingle Bells."

"What's that?" Nick Marino shouted from the room next door.

"Let's get out of here!" hissed Frank.

Above the sound of the robot, the brothers heard the door slam in the next room and footsteps in the hall.

Staggering blindly in the dark, guided by the light of the moon, Frank found his way back to the window. He could hear Joe's footsteps behind him.

He climbed out the window and jumped down. He was met by Larry, who had heard the robot and ran over from his lookout spot. Together they waited for Joe to appear at the window.

"I don't get it," Frank said. He looked up at the window. "He was right behind me!"

Frank and Larry kept looking at the window, expecting Joe to come bursting through at any second. "Joe?" Frank called softly.

They saw the light go on in the room.

Frank's heart sank. Joe was trapped!

8 Blowout!

A second after the light went on, it went off again, along with the light in the hallway.

From his hiding place behind a stack of boxes, Joe heard Marino say, "It's those fuses again! The wiring in this old firetrap stinks!"

"I'll go downstairs and replace the fuse," the woman said nervously. Joe heard her hurry out of the room.

Then he heard something move at his feet. He lifted one foot, then put it down again. As soon as he did, a loud screech filled the room.

Joe looked down. A black-and-white cat arched its back at him, spat, and then darted for the lighted doorway. "Dice, you crazy cat," Marino said, almost affectionately. "*You're* the one who knocked over the robot."

Joe held his breath. Since Marino seemed to think that Dice was responsible for starting the robot, maybe he could escape now.

No such luck. He heard Marino continue to walk slowly through the room.

"Might as well get that set of old toy soldiers Brannigan wanted," muttered Marino.

Joe could hear him coming closer. Marino's eyes had probably adjusted to the dark by now. Joe was pretty sure the man would see him if he started looking near the boxes.

Joe decided to take a chance and crawl toward the window. If he could get there quickly enough, he could climb out before Marino had a chance to nail him.

He dropped to the floor as quietly as he could and began to creep toward the window. Marino's footsteps were getting closer and closer. Suddenly, Joe's hand touched something soft and hairy. For a few seconds he froze, before realizing it was a gorilla mask made out of rubber and artificial hair.

Marino was almost on top of him. Without thinking, Joe quickly pulled the mask on over his head and shrank back against the wall, his hands behind his back. He held his breath and waited, hoping that, in the darkness, Marino would think he was a life-sized stuffed doll.

Marino passed by Joe, glancing at him briefly. Then he walked over to a shelf a few feet away. "Here it is," Marino said. He lifted something off the shelf. Then he left the room, shutting the door behind him.

Joe began to breathe easily again. Playing

gorilla statue had worked. He took off the mask and headed for the window. He climbed out, then dropped back down to the ground.

"Are you all right?" Frank whispered anxiously. "What happened up there?"

"Oh, not much," Joe said, grinning. "I was just auditioning for the lead in a remake of *King Kong*, that's all!" Then he added, "I'll tell you about it later. Right now, I think we ought to get out of here."

"Right," agreed Frank. "Before Marino decides he needs some fresh air."

The Hardys and Larry headed for the van.

On their way back to the motel, Frank said, "I wonder what Marino meant, about moving to the museum if anything went wrong."

"Well, we all know what the woman meant about 'getting to the old man through the kid,'" Larry said bitterly.

"She also mentioned the name Marc," said Joe. "Setting you up must have been Delaney's idea."

Frank pulled into the motel parking lot and stopped beside Larry's convertible.

"Thanks for letting me come with you," Larry said to Frank and Joe, as he got into his car. He looked up at them. "By the way, who is the missing witness you mentioned back there?"

Frank told him about the anonymous phone caller and the ledger, adding, "He's the only one who can nail Brannigan and Delaney. Dad has to find him!"

"Well, I hope he turns up soon," Larry replied. "For everybody's sake." He said good night to the Hardys and drove off.

The brothers went back to their room.

"It's too late to do any studying now," Joe said with a yawn. He looked over at his brother and smiled. Frank was lying on his bed, on top of the covers, fast asleep.

Before leaving for breakfast the next morning, Frank tried calling Fenton, but there was no answer. As soon as Frank replaced the receiver, the phone rang. Frank answered it, expecting to hear his father on the other end. Instead, a hushed, mysterious voice asked, "So, what are you guys doing in Philadelphia?"

"Get serious, Chet!" Frank said, immediately recognizing the voice of a friend from Bayport. "I know it's you!"

"How'd you know it was me?" Chet Morton asked in a surprised tone. Before Frank could reply, Chet added, "Your mom gave me your number, by the way."

"Look, Chet, Joe and I have to leave in a minute," Frank said. "What's up?"

"I'm coming down to Philly this afternoon," Chet said. "New York is playing Philadelphia. Can you and Joe make the game?"

The Hardys had the afternoon off because of

a staff meeting at the academy. Frank relayed Chet's message to Joe. After discussing whether or not they should spend their free time studying, investigating, or going to the game, the brothers decided they could use some fun and relaxation. Frank told Chet they'd meet him at Veterans Stadium at one o'clock.

"Great!" said Chet. "Meet me at the ticket booth."

Later, at breakfast in a diner near the academy, Joe retrieved a copy of the newspaper that had been left by a customer on the next table. He turned to the financial section.

"There's been another takeover in the game industry," Joe told his brother. He handed Frank the paper and pointed to the item.

Frank read that Consolidated Toys, one of the nation's largest amusement companies, with headquarters in Philadelphia, had just been taken over by Happy Times, Limited, a new toy and game conglomerate.

"These takeovers seem to be happening pretty fast," Frank commented. "But what do they have to do with us?"

Joe shrugged. "I don't know. Maybe I've just got toys on my mind because of that store."

When they got to the academy, the first thing the Hardys heard was that Larry Crawford was in trouble again.

"What kind of trouble?" Frank asked cadet Mike Cordero, who had told them the news.

He wondered when Larry had had time to get into trouble, since he and Joe had been out with him until about one in the morning, and it was only eight the next morning now.

"Some ammunition and two police pistols were missing from the arms room," Mike told them. "They were found this morning, in Larry's locker. He's being questioned by Lieutenant Redpath now."

"It wouldn't have been hard for someone to plant the ammo and weapons in Larry's locker," Joe told his brother as they headed for class. "Someone around here knows how to play with combination locks."

When classes were over, Frank and Joe saw Larry storming down the hall, muttering angrily to himself.

"Redpath must have really chewed him out," Joe said.

"I just hope Redpath didn't *kick* him out," Frank said worriedly.

As they headed for their van they saw Larry walk over to a sports car and get in on the passenger side. A very pretty blond girl was behind the wheel. The brothers also noticed Dennis Fielding standing near the car. A look of jealous hatred flashed across Fielding's pale, thin face as he watched the girl speed off with Larry.

"Maybe *she's* the reason Fielding is after Larry," Joe suggested. "And that would mean that O'Connor could be the only one who's working for Brannigan. He might know about Larry and the girl, and he's using that to get Fielding upset at Larry."

"Could be," Frank agreed. He looked at his watch. "But we don't really have time to talk about it now," he told Joe. "We have exactly ten minutes to get to the stadium to meet Chet."

The brothers made it to Veterans Stadium with two minutes to spare.

Chet was in the ticket line, munching on a hot dog. He was a heavyset teen who liked to eat. But despite his bulk, Chet was good at sports, especially football. His favorite sport, however, was baseball.

"So what *are* you guys doing in Philly, anyway?" Chet asked as they walked up to their seats in the grandstand.

"Oh, we're just taking some course our dad suggested," Frank said casually.

"Sure you are," Chet said slyly. "Okay, you guys don't have to tell me if you don't want to." He paused for a moment. Then he said, "So what kind of case are you working on?"

Joe tried changing the subject. "I hear it's going to be a real pitching duel today. What do you think of the match-up, Chet?"

That did the trick. Chet launched into a long explanation about the starting pitchers, their statistics, and who was likely to appear in relief. The subject of what Frank and Joe were doing in Philadelphia never came up again.

During the game, Frank and Joe tried to concentrate on each play, but it wasn't easy. They couldn't stop thinking about the Brannigan case.

Finally, the low-run game ended, and the three friends stood up to leave.

"We've played more exciting ball in Bayport," Joe said.

"Definitely," said Chet. "Hey, maybe we should bring the Bayport Bombers to Philly for an exhibition game!"

"Or to New York," Frank added with a grin. "Both teams looked like they weren't concentrating very hard on the game today."

"Like us," Joe murmured. Chet shot him a look but didn't say anything.

As they filed out of the stadium, Joe suddenly spotted two familiar faces in the crowd. He nudged Frank and motioned toward the two men. Frank looked over to catch sight of Dennis Fielding and Sergeant O'Connor talking together in another line exiting the stadium. Neither Hardy thought that the sergeant or the cadet had spotted them in the dense crowd.

"I'll be right back," Chet said suddenly. "I want to get a soda before the concession closes."

When Chet was out of earshot, Joe frowned

and said, "Why do I get the feeling Fielding and O'Connor are talking about Larry?"

"Well, I don't think they're talking about the ballgame!" Frank responded.

"They have to be working together to set up Larry," stated Joe. "It's just too much of a coincidence—an instructor and a cadet going to a ball game together."

Frank nodded. "Especially *that* instructor and *that* cadet!"

Just then, Chet caught up to them, a cup of soda in his hand. The Hardys tried to find some excuse to leave Chet, so they could follow O'Connor and Fielding. But they couldn't. Chet wanted to do some sight-seeing before going back to Bayport.

"Why don't we take my car?" suggested Chet.

Just then, the Hardys saw Fielding and O'Connor get into a green sedan. Sergeant O'Connor got behind the wheel.

"Oh, I'd rather take the van, okay, Chet?" Frank said quickly.

Chet started to protest, but Frank and Joe sprinted off toward the van. Chet shrugged and followed them.

As soon as Chet had climbed into the back of the van, Frank began tailing O'Connor and Fielding. Joe played tour guide, trying to distract Chet by naming sights of interest. But every so often he would glance at O'Connor's car. Frank choked back a laugh when he realized that some of the historic buildings Joe was pointing out were made up.

After a few minutes, O'Connor pulled his car up to a curb and stopped. Frank parked the van a short distance behind them. "Hey!" Chet said in a protesting voice. "What are we stopping for?" He narrowed his eyes. "You're not going to tell me there's something historic about this barber shop, are you?" he said suspiciously.

All of a sudden, the black sports car belonging to Nick Marino pulled up alongside O'Connor's car. There were two men in Marino's car.

Marino got out of the passenger side of the car and into the backseat of O'Connor's car. The sergeant drove off in a burn of rubber. The driver of the black sports car made an illegal U-turn and sped away in the opposite direction.

Frank started up the van again and followed O'Connor's car.

"I get it," Chet said, nodding. "You're following that green sedan, right?"

"Look, Chet, we've got a lot of studying to do for our course," Frank said. "Why don't I let you out at the next traffic light? Then you can get a cab back to your car."

"Forget it!" replied Chet. "I'm in on your case now, whether you like it or not! *Whatever* it is," he added, glaring at them.

"Don't look now," Joe said suddenly, "but *we're* being followed!"

Frank glanced in his side-view mirror and saw the black sports car on their tail. He looked ahead again and saw O'Connor start onto a small bridge over the Schuylkill River. Frank followed the green sedan onto the bridge.

An instant later, the speeding black car came alongside the van and began to scrape its left side, nudging it toward the outer edge of the road on the bridge.

"Nice guy," mumbled Chet.

Suddenly the van began to swerve, causing Chet to lose his balance and tumble to the floor. He scrambled to his knees and gripped the back of Joe's seat.

Alarmed, Chet looked out of the window. Far below, he saw a tugboat plying the river.

With a sickening thump, the black car swiped them again. Frank gripped the wheel hard in a desperate attempt to steady the van.

"How about getting me that cab you were talking about?" Chet gulped, as he tried to keep from falling onto the floor again.

Knowing that it was impossible to outrace the other vehicle, Frank tried to turn the van to the left and get away from the edge of the bridge. But the driver of the black sports car kept swerving back and forth, banging into the left side of the van harder each time.

85

"I'm losing control of the wheel!" Frank shouted.

Joe grabbed hold of the dashboard and braced himself with both hands.

They heard a loud bang, and the van barrelled toward the guard rail along the edge of the bridge.

"Oh, no!" Chet cried. "We're going over!"

9 Wild Shots

Frank gritted his teeth and turned the wheel hard to the left; he slammed on the brakes. They all heard the crunch of metal as the right side of the van scraped against the metal guard rail. The van spun around to the left and stopped.

Joe looked out the window and saw the black car and the green sedan speeding ahead down the road.

"Both of you okay?" Frank said breathlessly.

"Fine," said Joe. His seat belt had held him against the force of the sudden stop.

"Chet?" asked Frank, turning around.

"I'm okay," Chet replied. He got to his knees and leaned against Joe's seat. "I should have known that sight-seeing with you guys would end up in a car chase!"

"I wonder who was driving Marino's car," said Joe, after he had caught his breath.

"Probably another one of Brannigan's goons." Frank opened his door. "We better check to see if there's any damage to the van."

The brothers jumped out of the van. Chet followed, more slowly.

Joe looked at the left rear tire. "Flat," he said, giving the tire a kick.

Frank looked up the road. "It's a good thing there isn't any traffic on this bridge." He opened up the back of the van and lifted out the spare tire.

After Frank and Joe had changed the tire, they dropped Chet off at his car and then drove back to the police academy to do some looking around.

"If O'Connor is working for Brannigan, maybe we can find something in his office that will prove it," Frank said.

"What about that missing ledger?" Joe suggested. "Maybe O'Connor's keeping it at the academy. An office in the academy might be the perfect place to stash it. No one would ever think of looking there."

"No one except us." Frank started walking in the direction of O'Connor's office.

The main building at the academy was deserted. The Hardys' footsteps echoed against the tiled floor.

When they got to Sergeant O'Connor's office, they knocked first, to check if anyone was inside. After a moment, Frank tried the knob.

The door was locked. Joe took a plastic card from his wallet, slid it between the door and the lock, and wedged the lock back. He pushed the door open a crack and peered inside.

"Empty," Joe said.

"He's probably still with Fielding and Marino."

Frank turned on the lights, closed the door, and examined O'Connor's desk. He pulled open the long top drawer. "Joe!" he exclaimed. "Look at this."

Joe hurried over to his brother. Half-hidden under a pile of test papers was the butt end of a service pistol.

"Weapons aren't supposed to be left unattended," Frank said. "They're kept in a locked vault in the arms room."

He looked at his brother. "So what's this one doing in O'Connor's office? I wonder if it connects O'Connor with the weapons and ammo Larry is accused of stealing."

Suddenly the door swung open and a voice asked gruffly, "What are you two doing in here?"

The brothers turned and saw Lieutenant Redpath standing in the doorway.

"We . . . uh . . . had something to ask Sarge," Frank stammered. "His . . . uh . . . door was open, so we thought he might be working late."

"He has the afternoon off," Redpath said, looking at them suspiciously. "Why are you both here? I should think you'd have wanted to get away for the day, like all the other cadets."

The Hardys wondered if Redpath had seen the pistol in the drawer, which was still open. If he had, he obviously wasn't saying anything about it.

"Anything I can do for you instead?" he asked coldly.

"We just wondered . . . how we scored on the Constitutional law test this morning," Joe said quickly.

Good thinking, Joe, thought Frank.

"Neither of you did very well," Redpath snapped. "You're both going to have to do a lot better—that is, *if* you expect to remain cadets and graduate. I told you, you might find it easy getting in, but staying in will be a lot tougher."

Redpath turned and walked toward the door. Joe quickly and quietly closed the drawer.

"Well, see you tomorrow," Redpath said, holding the door open for them.

Frank and Joe walked past him out of the office.

They heard Redpath close the door behind them and lock it. Outside, on their way to the van, Joe said, "Why was Redpath the only one around?"

"He didn't look like he knew about the pistol in O'Connor's desk," Frank said. "But he might have already known it was there."

"So was it O'Connor's pistol or one from the arms room?" Joe asked.

Frank shook his head and shrugged. Then he said, "I think it's time to tell Dad what's going on."

They drove back to the motel. Inside their room, they phoned Fenton at his hotel room. This time he was in.

Frank filled his father in on everything that had happened since they had last seen him.

Fenton listened carefully. When Frank had finished, he pronounced his verdict. "It sounds like the two cases are linked. That doesn't make me very happy. These guys are dangerous. But now that you're involved in the Brannigan business, I guess there's no keeping you out of it. Just watch your backs, all right?"

"We've been in dangerous situations before," Frank reminded his father. "But we promise to play it extra careful this time."

"I'm going to be at the police academy tomorrow," Fenton said. "There's a shooting demonstration at the pistol range. Commissioner Crawford will be there too. He thinks it'll be a good opportunity for me to look around."

"Are we supposed to recognize you?" Frank asked.

"Absolutely not," answered Fenton. "It might tip our hand."

"But Marino already knows we're involved. O'Connor and Fielding may know, too."

"Perhaps so. But they may not know you're related to me, or that we're working together. I'd like to keep it that way."

Frank tried to sound cheerful as he said good night to his father. But inside, he was worried.

After lunch the next day, Frank and Joe joined the other recruits at the pistol range for the demonstration. Larry and Dennis's class would be firing at targets while the others watched.

Inside the pistol range building, the brothers saw their father standing with a group of spectators. They saw Commissioner Crawford, too, on the other side of the room.

"I guess they've agreed not to recognize each other," Joe said to Frank.

The Hardys watched closely as Larry and Dennis took turns firing at stationary targets. First they fired from twenty-five feet away, then fifty, then seventy-five.

"They seem to be scoring about the same," Joe concluded after checking the scoreboard behind the cadets.

Frank looked at his father. As he did, he saw something punch a small hole in the wall right next to Fenton Hardy's head. Frank realized that someone had just fired a bullet at his father!

At the same moment the firing stopped, another shot rang out. Frank looked in the direction he thought the shot had come from and then back to his father. Now Fenton was nowhere in sight.

Everyone started talking at once.

"Somebody just tried to shoot Dad twice," Frank said to his brother. "I saw the first shot hit the wall behind him."

"What?" exclaimed Joe, who spun around, trying to locate their father.

Suddenly, Fenton reappeared in the doorway. He looked over at his sons and gave them a slight nod. Frank and Joe sighed with relief. It was obvious Fenton knew what had happened and was taking every precaution.

Frank glanced over at Dennis Fielding. He was standing completely still, his mouth open. A voice came over the loudspeaker announcing that a wild bullet had been fired, but that no one was hurt.

"The first shot at Dad was under the cover of the pistol-firing demonstration. They figured with all the noise, no one would notice," Frank said.

"And if Dad got hit, they would have thought it was a ricochet from the 'wild bullet,'" Joe said.

Later, after all the pistols had been checked

93

in, Lieutenant Redpath announced that the wild shot was an accident, probably just a ricochet.

"This shooting business doesn't add up," Frank said to Joe. "Redpath says it's a ricochet, but I don't believe it. Is he trying to cover up for someone, or for the academy?"

"We'll just have to keep working on it," Joe replied.

That evening, watching the news on TV, the brothers discovered they weren't the only ones wondering about a cover-up at the police academy.

A TV reporter held a microphone in front of Marcus Delaney.

"Would you care to comment on today's shooting incident at the police academy?" the reporter asked.

"As far as I'm concerned, it's the last straw!" Delaney said angrily. "I've been saying for a long time now that Commissioner Crawford runs a Mickey Mouse police department. Crime is rampant in the streets. It's not surprising that citizens aren't safe anymore, if this is the way our policemen are trained!"

"He's sure taking advantage of the situation," commented Joe.

"I guess he has to, to get what he wants," Frank replied. "But I doubt if Crawford and the D.A. will drop the grand jury investigation, even after today."

Frank and Joe turned their attention back to the television.

"Commissioner Crawford should be investigated, not my client!" Delaney was saying. "The commissioner has lost control of the police department and the police academy. Now he's attempting to cover up what happened today at the academy pistol range. Someone might have gotten hurt!"

"He's right about that," murmured Joe, thinking of his father and the bullet that had just missed him.

"Why would the commissioner want to cover up something that could have been an accident?" the reporter asked.

"It would bring about an investigation that might cost him his job," Delaney insisted. "It would reveal mismanagement the public doesn't know about. Like the favoritism the commissioner is showing to his grandson, a cadet at the academy. Every infraction of the rules committed by his grandson has been covered up. And that includes cheating on exams and stealing weapons and ammunition!"

"Those are pretty serious accusations," the reporter said. "Can you back them up?"

"Ask Lieutenant Redpath at the police academy, if you don't believe me," Delaney retorted. "I tell you, the commissioner is incompetent! He can't even run his own police academy, and he's playing favorites by not having his grandson expelled. The commissioner ought to clean up his own act, instead of trying to discredit innocent businessmen like Jack Brannigan!"

"It all fits together now," Frank said as he and Joe tore into the roast beef sandwiches, fries, and sodas they had bought at the deli. "Delaney's plan is to get the commissioner fired. With Crawford gone, the grand jury investigation would be delayed."

Joe nodded. "Delayed indefinitely, if Delaney can manage it. And he's such a good lawyer, he might be able to do it."

"It's a clever strategy," Frank said. "If it works. Our job is to help Dad see that it doesn't work."

"If we could just find that witness and the ledger," Joe said, "then we could wrap up this case."

The phone rang. Frank picked it up.

"I just finished meeting with the commissioner," Fenton told him. "I want you two to meet me at my hotel. We need to talk."

"We're on our way," Frank replied.

Driving downtown in the van, the brothers went back over what they knew.

"I still haven't made up my mind about

Redpath yet," Frank said. "But I think it's more likely O'Connor was responsible for the warning note and the shooting incident."

"But not Fielding," Joe added. "Somehow, I can't see him going that far to get Larry expelled."

Frank agreed. "He looked really surprised by the wild shot."

They pulled into the hotel's parking veranda, left the van with an attendant, and took the elevator up to the seventh floor. Frank knocked on Fenton's door. There was no reply.

Frank rapped harder on the door. But there was still no answer from inside the room.

"Dad?" Joe called, banging on the door. He tried the door, but it was locked.

"Maybe something came up," Frank suggested. "Let's go back to the motel and see if he's left a message."

Before leaving the hotel they checked at the front desk to see if their father had left a message. But there was none. They retrieved the van and started back for the Liberty Bell Lodge.

"This isn't like Dad," Joe said, as they pulled into the motel. "He'd have left a message, or found some other way to tell us where he'd gone."

"Maybe he didn't call us from his room," Frank said.

97

That made sense to Joe. "He might have called from someplace where he was following up a lead."

"What's that on the floor?" Joe asked when they had stepped into their room.

Frank picked up a folded piece of paper. He unfolded it and read it quickly. Then he crumpled the note and threw it angrily against the wall. He turned and stormed toward the window.

"What did you do that for?" Joe said, startled at seeing his brother act this way.

Frank stared out the window. He took a slow, deep breath and said, "Dad's been kidnapped!"

10 Where Is Fenton Hardy?

Joe quickly scooped up the kidnap note, unfolded it, and began to read. The note said: "Don't keep nosing around, or we'll kill your father."

Joe studied the handwriting on the note. "Practically illegible. Just like the warning note. Both notes were probably written by the same person—whoever that is."

Meanwhile, Frank had calmed down. He turned away from the window and looked at his brother.

"So what do we do now?" Joe asked Frank anxiously. "We've got to find Dad!"

"First we call the commissioner," Frank said, picking up the phone.

Commissioner Crawford answered on the first ring.

"We just found a kidnap note at our motel," Frank told him. "They've got Dad!"

99

"I'll put a special team to work searching for him," Commissioner Crawford said reassuringly. "Don't worry, we'll find your father. Stay out of it for now. I suggest you stick to your work at the police academy."

After telling Joe what the commissioner had said, Frank shook his head. "We can't just sit back and do nothing while Dad's in danger."

"The toy store!" Joe said suddenly. "I bet that's where they took Dad."

Frank nodded. "Let's go!"

Frank drove the van as fast as he could to the store. When they got there they checked the rear of the building. This time there were no lights on upstairs. The place was deserted.

"We've got to think," Frank said, quickly climbing into the driver's seat and shoving the key into the ignition. "Where else could they have taken Dad?"

"What about the museum Marino mentioned?" said Joe.

"*What* museum?" Frank asked, reaching into the glove compartment and pulling out a map of Philadelphia. "There are a lot of museums in Philadelphia. Anyway, maybe it's not a museum at all. Maybe 'museum' is a code word for something else."

"I hate to admit it," Joe said, "but we may have hit a dead end."

Frank bit his lip and thought for a minute.

100

Then he said, "I think it's time for a showdown with Sergeant O'Connor."

"That suits me fine, but how are we going to find him? We don't know where he lives."

"Let's try the police academy," Frank suggested. "They're holding night classes. Maybe he's instructing one of them." He looked at Joe. "Larry and Dennis Fielding might be there, too. Larry and Dennis both started patrol training tonight. They're riding in patrol cars with a supervisor. Next week they'll be walking beats during the day."

When the Hardys reached the academy, they saw Sergeant O'Connor's green sedan parked in the lot. Frank drove back out of the lot and parked the van across the street. There, they had a good view of the brightly lit parking lot and O'Connor's car.

After fifteen minutes on the stakeout, they saw O'Connor hurry to his car and drive it out of the lot.

Frank pulled the van away from the curb and followed O'Connor.

The sergeant headed southeast, toward the Delaware River.

"Is he going into New Jersey?" Frank wondered.

O'Connor turned onto a dimly lit, tree-lined street. He slowed down, then stopped next to a huge Victorian-style house.

101

Frank parked the van behind a truck half a block away. He and Joe got out of the van and watched as O'Connor stepped out of his car. He walked briskly to the house, pausing briefly to look in a window.

"Nice house," Joe commented. "But isn't it a little big?"

Frank shrugged. "Maybe it's been converted into apartments. Or maybe O'Connor has a big family."

A moment later O'Connor walked around to the back of the building. Frank and Joe quietly followed at a safe distance.

They saw the sergeant stop at the back door. He tapped on the door softly. It opened, and O'Connor went inside.

"We've got to get into the house," Frank said.

Frank and Joe walked to the front of the house, looking for a way in. Suddenly Frank spotted a sign attached to the wall next to the door. He quietly sneaked up the porch steps, Joe following.

"'Evans's Antique Toy Museum,'" read Frank.

"Just what we're looking for—a museum," whispered Joe.

The brothers left the porch and went around to the other side of the house. Halfway toward the back, Frank saw a small basement window.

"It might be big enough for us to crawl through," he said. "If it isn't locked."

Joe tried raising the window, but it was stuck. He took his Swiss Army knife out of his pants pocket and began to dig away at the paint that filled the crack between the window and the sill.

After a few minutes, Joe tried the window again. It wouldn't budge. Frank lent a hand, and after a tremendous yank it began to give. They opened it as far as it could go and crawled inside. The basement was dark, and there was a strong smell of mothballs.

Once their eyes had adjusted to the darkness, Frank and Joe could see an assortment of old-fashioned toys. There were rocking horses, toy soldiers, and elaborately made doll houses.

"Look at those hula hoops and pogo sticks," Joe said. "They were real popular toys in the 1950s and '60s."

"We don't have time to do any sightseeing now," Frank said impatiently. He pulled his brother away from a display case containing old-time baseball cards. "We have to find Dad!"

They walked around the basement, looking for the stairs to the first floor. Frank went down one side of the room, Joe the other. Suddenly Joe came to a door. He turned the knob and opened the door slowly. He pushed open the door farther and stepped forward into the darkness. He barely heard the click of the door as it closed behind him.

In the darkness, Joe felt an arm grab him around the neck. Before he could yell for help, another hand clamped over his mouth.

He heard a raspy voice murmur in his ear, "Don't worry, kid. I'm taking you to see your father—for the last time!"

11 Clues and a Confession

Meanwhile, Frank had spotted a door on his side of the basement. He opened it and walked into a small room. The room was dimly lit by an old-fashioned kerosene lamp, and it was empty except for a card table and some chairs.

Frank approached the table; he saw that someone had been playing a game of Monopoly. The board and pieces looked very old.

This game has got to be a first edition, Frank thought.

He saw a small orange card lying on the floor. He picked it up. It was the Get Out of Jail Free card from the game.

Frank turned the card over, but it was blank.

Frank looked on the floor but could find no more Monopoly cards. The rest of the cards were stacked neatly on top of the game board. "I wonder if someone dropped that card deliberately," he muttered.

He left the room to tell Joe about his discovery, but when he got back to the basement, his brother was gone.

"Joe!" called Frank. When his brother didn't answer, Frank began to worry.

He searched the basement and found another door. He opened it and stepped inside. As he did, he tripped over something. He bent down, picked up the object, and gasped.

It was one of Joe's sneakers.

Frank groped around the wall for a light switch. He found it and flicked it on. The room was flooded with light, but Joe Hardy was nowhere to be seen.

He shut the light off and hurried out of the room, climbed back out the basement window, and raced for the van. Using the cellular phone, he dialed Commissioner Crawford's number.

"Now Joe's missing," Frank said as soon as the commissioner answered the phone.

"I'll notify my special team immediately," Crawford said. "Frank, you go back to your motel and get some rest. Let the police find your father and brother. Two Hardys missing is enough. I don't want a third disappearing."

Before Frank hung up the phone, he asked the commissioner for Larry's phone number. The commissioner gave it to him. Frank thanked him and hung up. Then he picked up the phone again and dialed Larry's number.

He hoped Larry had finished patrol training for the night and had gone home.

Fortunately, Larry answered on the first ring. Frank excitedly told him what had happened. He felt he would burst inside from the frustration of losing both Fenton and Joe. Larry calmed Frank down.

"Let's figure out our next move, Frank."

"My next move is to pay a little visit to Dennis Fielding," replied Frank. "Do you have his address?"

"Sure," replied Larry. "But what do you want it for?"

"Right now, he's my only lead," Frank said. "He's *got* to know something that will help me find Dad and Joe."

Larry gave Frank the address. "I'll go back to the academy and take a look around. I'll give you a call later. Let me know what else I can do to help then." He hung up.

Frank drove to the address Larry had given him. Dennis lived in a large brick apartment building near the police academy. Frank parked the van across the street, got out, and walked to the building.

Inside the foyer, he found Dennis Fielding's name on the mailbox. Frank pressed the buzzer and waited, but there was no answer. He tried the buzzer again several times without success.

There was only one thing to do: go back to the van and wait for Dennis to show up.

An hour passed, then two hours. Frank yawned and looked at his watch. It was after three A.M. His eyes felt heavy. He was falling asleep.

Then he jerked up his head, suddenly wide awake. Marino's black sports car was pulling up in front of Dennis's building. Frank watched as Dennis got out of the car and headed up the walk. Marino sped away.

Frank jumped out of the van and ran up to Dennis, catching him at the door. Dennis whirled around and stared at Frank.

Frank decided to take the offensive. He grabbed Dennis by the front of his shirt and said, "Okay, Fielding, it's time you and I had a little talk. I know exactly what you've been up to at the academy. You're in worse trouble now. Kidnapping and attempted murder is a major offense. You're going to jail for life!"

Dennis turned pale. Then a look of recognition swept across his face. "I've seen you at the academy. You're one of the new cadets." He shook his head. "Listen, I don't know what you're talking about. I never kidnapped anybody!"

"You're lying," Frank said angrily, tightening his hold on the cadet.

Dennis looked at Frank, then he said, "Okay, okay, maybe you'd better come up."

Frank let Dennis go. Dennis straightened his shirt. Then he led the way into the building.

When they got to his apartment on the fourth floor, Dennis immediately flopped in an easy chair.

"Now, what's this all about?" he asked.

"My father and brother have been kidnapped," Frank said, standing over him. "You know that. And we both know Jack Brannigan's behind it. When he goes to trial for kidnapping, among other things, *you'll* go with him, as an accomplice or an accessory. Like your pals O'Connor and Marino. So maybe you ought to tell me what you know."

Dennis suddenly caved in. He looked at Frank, his face as white as a sheet.

"You know everything," Dennis said shakily. "Otherwise, I'd never tell you this. Marino just told me that Brannigan can't afford to let your father and brother go. That ledger was the wrong one. He figures if the guy he took won't tell him where the right ledger is, he may have told your father."

"My father's never even talked to the witness," Frank said, his voice rising.

"Brannigan doesn't know that. All he knows is that your father's on the case and might know where the ledger is. That's the way Brannigan is. He's like a bulldozer—he'll run over anyone he thinks can hurt him and snatch anyone who may know where that ledger is." Dennis fidgeted in his chair as Frank paced back and forth.

Frank looked at Dennis sitting dejectedly in his chair. The cadet looked totally miserable.

"Okay," Frank said, sitting down. "Why don't you just tell me your story?"

"What do you want to know?" Dennis asked with a sigh.

"First of all, why did you and Larry stop being friends?"

Dennis looked at Frank. "I used to date a girl named Gail—until she met Larry. In fact, I introduced her to Larry. After that, I was history as far as she was concerned. I got jealous of him," Dennis admitted.

"And it seemed like the instructors were always treating him as if he were something special. They'd go easier on him than on me or the other cadets just because he was the commissioner's grandson. Now I don't think they really did, but it seemed that way to me then, after I lost Gail."

"But you were friends," Frank said. "You could have told him how you felt."

Dennis looked down at the floor. "I know," he replied with a nod. "But he's got that fancy convertible, and he wears those expensive clothes." Dennis paused a moment, then he added, "I don't know. It all started getting to me."

"How did O'Connor get you to help him set up Larry?" asked Frank.

"It didn't take much," Dennis said, smiling

grimly. "O'Connor could see something was bothering me. I told him what was happening between Gail and me. Then he found out I had cheated on a couple of exams. I was too upset at the time to bother studying.

"He threatened to go to Redpath unless I helped him. At first I thought O'Connor just had some private grudge against Larry." Dennis shook his head sadly. "By the time I found out it was Brannigan I was *really* working for, it was too late. I was in it too deeply to get out."

"Where did you go with Marino last night?" Frank asked.

"That's part of Brannigan's game. He gets his hatchetmen to play with your head, scare you. Anything he thinks will work. They blindfolded me, drove me around, took me to some weird place." Frank noticed Dennis's hands trembling. "It was a scare tactic; they wanted me to step up the pressure on Larry."

Frank *had* to know where Marino had taken Dennis. "What about sounds and smells? Maybe you heard something along the way that can help me figure out where they took you. Think! While you were riding in the car—did someone say something or did you hear anything?"

"I only heard traffic sounds," Dennis said. He thought for a moment. "Wait a minute, I just remembered something."

"What?" Frank said, leaning closer.

"The building they took me to was drafty and damp. I thought it might have been a warehouse. They left me alone for a few minutes and it was really quiet. I remember hearing the crack of a baseball bat. Kids cheering. There must have been a ball game going on nearby."

"Good!" Frank said. He jumped to his feet. "Did you hear anything else besides a ball game?"

Fielding thought again. "We must have been near a river. I heard a tugboat horn."

"*Which* river?" Frank asked. "Philly is between *two* rivers!"

Dennis shook his head slowly. "I don't know which one."

"The Schuylkill on the west, or the Delaware on the east?" Frank asked desperately.

Fielding shrugged. "I was blindfolded, remember?"

Frank thought for a moment. "It was the river closest to where some baseball game was being played last night. The Phillies were off last night, so it wasn't Veterans Stadium." He looked at Dennis. "I've got to find that warehouse, and you've got to come with me."

Fielding agreed to go with Frank. They left the apartment building and got into the van. Frank drove to the nearest gas station, stopped, and filled up the tank.

112

"Wonder if you can help us," Frank said to the attendant. "We're trying to find a ballpark. Near one of the rivers. *Not* Veterans Stadium."

The attendant scratched his head with a greasy hand and yawned. "Isn't six A.M. a little early in the morning for a ball game?"

"It's important," Frank told the young man. "Do you know if there's a ballpark near one of the rivers? Someplace where they play night games?"

The attendant thought a moment. "The only ballpark near one of the rivers where they play night games that I know of is Franklin Field Stadium, near the University of Pennsylvania. Just across the Schuylkill River from Schuylkill River Park."

Frank thanked the attendant, paid him, and drove away. "The warehouse has to be around there somewhere," he told Dennis. "Near the park just across from the stadium on this side of the river."

Frank drove west. Soon they were driving along the Schuylkill riverfront on South Street.

Frank turned onto a side street and drove slowly toward Schuylkill River Park.

The foghorn of a tugboat blared. Across the river, Frank and Dennis could see the high walls of Franklin Field Stadium, on the University of Pennsylvania campus.

"Now all we have to do is find the warehouse," Frank said.

113

But there was no warehouse anywhere in sight.

Frank drove through the entire neighborhood that surrounded the park but came up empty. He was driving back toward the river when he noticed an old red-brick building near the north end of the park.

"This looks like a warehouse to me," Frank said as he parked the van on a side street a short way from the building. He and Dennis got out.

The warehouse looked deserted. Cobwebs covered the windows, and weeds grew up around the sides of the building.

"All the windows have bars on them," Dennis pointed out. "We can't get in through any of them."

"And the front door would be too risky if they're in there. We'll have to take our chances around the back," Frank added.

Dennis followed Frank around to the back of the building, where they found a steel door. Frank slowly tried the knob. To his relief, it turned easily. Slowly, he opened the heavy door and stepped inside. Dennis followed. They stumbled in the dark until they came to another door. Frank slowly pushed it open. The door creaked loudly.

Frank and Dennis stepped through the door. The first person they saw was Nick Marino. Next to him was the saleswoman from the toy

114

store. They were sitting at a table close to the door. They looked up, startled. Near them, in chairs, with their hands tied behind them, were Fenton, Joe, and another man Frank didn't recognize.

Marino stood up and started toward Frank. He lunged at Frank, who sidestepped him neatly. Marino fell past him onto a tall, empty crate, overturning it.

A kerosene lamp, which had been resting on the crate, fell over onto a tall stack of old newspapers. In seconds, a wall of fire blazed up, cutting them all off from the exit door.

12 To Atlantic City

Nick Marino staggered back from the flames. Then he darted past Frank, back to the woman and the captives. Marino hauled Fenton Hardy out of his chair and pulled the bound detective to his feet.

The woman pulled the third prisoner upright. She and Marino headed for the rear of the warehouse, dragging their captives with them.

"They must be heading for the front door!" Dennis said.

But Frank had a worse problem. His brother was still tied up in the path of the quickly spreading fire. Glancing around, Frank found some heavy mover's blankets. He tossed some to Dennis Fielding. Together, they smothered the fire.

Frank rushed over to his brother and untied

him. Joe pulled the gag out of his mouth and cried, "We have to go after them. Quick!"

They ran through the warehouse, reaching the entrance just in time to see Marino's black sports car speeding away.

"We'll never catch them," Dennis Fielding said, coming up behind the brothers.

"They'll probably head for another hiding place," Frank said. He looked at his brother. "At least we've got *you!*"

"What are *you* doing here?" Joe asked Dennis.

"After I discovered you were missing, I went to Dennis's apartment," explained Frank. He told Joe how Fielding had admitted his role in the Brannigan scheme and had helped Frank find the warehouse.

"I've decided to turn myself in," Dennis told the brothers when Frank had finished. "I can't take the pressure anymore." He laughed bitterly. "It's funny. All this time, Larry's been accused of things, but I was the one who was really messing up."

"Things will go much easier for you if you turn yourself in," Frank said. "And if we can help in any way, just let us know."

"Thanks, guys," Dennis said. "I really appreciate that."

Frank and Joe drove Dennis home. When the brothers were alone in the van again, Joe said, "You remember the other guy who was tied up in the warehouse? That was the missing witness."

"I figured that," Frank replied. Then he took the Get Out of Jail Free card out of his pocket and handed it to Joe.

"I found that on the floor in one of the rooms of the basement in the museum. Got any ideas who might have dropped it?"

Joe thought for a moment. Then he said, "I saw the witness drop something else while we were sitting in the warehouse. I'm positive it was a Monopoly card." He looked at Frank. "I even remember which one it was."

"Well?" Frank asked impatiently.

"It was the Water Works card," answered Joe.

"It's got to be a signal from the witness!" Frank exclaimed. "They must have been taken to the water works!"

Joe reached in the glove compartment for the map of Philadelphia.

"The water works are at the other end of town, by the Delaware River," Joe told his brother. "I'll direct you."

In less than half an hour, he and Frank had reached the block where the map said the Philadelphia water works was located.

Where the water works should have been was a construction site. Frank jumped out of the van and ran over to the site. He talked to a construction worker for a few minutes, then came back to the van.

"You won't believe this," he said to his brother. "The water works have been moved. To the Police Administration Building!"

Frank sat back in his seat and stared up at the roof of the van. "The Get Out of Jail Free card stumps me. And the Water Works card isn't leading us anywhere. Maybe the witness just dropped them by mistake."

They sat in silence for a moment. Then Frank murmured, "Do not pass Go. Do not collect two hundred dollars."

"That's it!" Joe exclaimed suddenly. He looked at his brother. "All the streets in Monopoly are named after streets in Atlantic City! It's not that far away, and Jack Brannigan has gambling connections there. *That's* where they took Dad and the witness! To the water works in Atlantic City!"

It was a long shot at best, but Frank admitted it was their only lead. They had to act on it. He started up the van again.

As Frank drove, Joe found an all-news station on the radio. The newscaster stated that the Philadelphia area would be under a thunderstorm alert for the next four to six hours.

As if on cue, rain started to pelt the van. Within minutes it was pouring.

"I can hardly see," Frank said, slowing the

van. "The windshield wipers are useless in this stuff."

"Maybe we should pull over and wait it out."

"Let's try to make it back to the motel," Frank said. "Larry might have come up with something at his end. We'll head out to Atlantic City as soon as the storm lets up. Besides, Marino and company may not go to Atlantic City until this storm blows over. They could be hiding out here in Philadelphia."

"I guess it's no use trying to track down their hiding place," Joe said dejectedly. "They could be anywhere in town."

A hard rain was still falling when the brothers got back to their motel, and they got drenched running the short distance from the van to their room.

As soon as they got inside the phone rang. Joe picked it up.

"It's Larry," he said to Frank. "He says he looked around the police academy for O'Connor but had no luck. He wants to know how things are going."

"So tell him," Frank said, as he peeled off his soaking T-shirt.

Joe told Larry everything that had happened since they had last seen him, finishing with their theory that Fenton and the witness were on the move to another hiding place, probably the water works in Atlantic City.

"We'd head there now, if it wasn't for the

storm. And the fact that we haven't had any sleep," Joe said. "But we're taking off as soon as the storm is over."

"I'm coming with you," Larry said. "I'll be at your place as soon as the storm blows over."

Before Joe had a chance to protest, Larry hung up.

"Larry insisted on coming with us," Joe told his brother.

"That's okay," replied Frank. "We might need the extra muscle anyway."

The Hardys ordered food from a nearby Chinese restaurant. When it came, they tore into it hungrily. Then they flopped on their beds and fell asleep instantly.

At about five o'clock the next morning, Frank and Joe were awakened by a loud knock on the door. A groggy Frank got up and opened it. "Ready?" Larry said with a grin.

"Give us a few minutes," Frank told him.

Larry stepped inside and waited while Frank woke up Joe and the two of them washed and dressed quickly.

All three of them piled into the van, heading toward Atlantic City. Joe played navigator, using their New Jersey road maps, finding the best route to help them get to Atlantic City as quickly as possible. They managed to cover the seventy-mile drive in a little over an hour.

Even though it was early in the morning, the

streets were choked with tourists. Joe spotted the water works on the city map. Frank followed Joe's directions, guiding the van through the heavy traffic. Above them loomed the giant hotels and casinos that lined Atlantic City's famous boardwalk.

The water works was located in a deserted section of the city.

"Why do I get the feeling this place hasn't been used as the water works for years?" asked Joe, as the three of them watched the wind blowing the weeds that surrounded the huge, run-down building.

"Let's check it out anyway," Frank said. "If you think about it, an abandoned building is the perfect place to hide someone you don't want found."

They got out of the van and walked to the building. A sign stuck into the ground near the sidewalk said, "Coming Soon! The Water Works Hotel and Casino. More Slots, More Fun!"

The three of them walked around the building, looking for a way in. Joe tried a large window. With a persuasive shove it opened easily, and they climbed through.

"This must have been the city's original water works," Larry said. "Look at all the old equipment."

The three of them began walking under a

maze of twisting pipes. "It's really quiet in here," whispered Frank.

"It's really *creepy* in here," Joe whispered back.

Suddenly a voice rang out of the darkness.

"Don't make another move!"

13 A Witness Sings

The Hardys and Larry whirled around. In the dim light, they saw a man standing ten feet away.

The man came toward Frank. He was tall and bearlike, and his face was unshaven. His clothes were old and worn.

Frank tensed, expecting him to charge. But the closer the man came, the more slowly he moved.

"What are you doing in here?" the man demanded. He sat down on a pipe and picked at his beard. "You're not cops, are you?"

"He must be homeless," Joe whispered to Frank.

"He probably lives here," Frank whispered back.

Frank looked at the man and smiled. "No, we're not policemen, sir," he said. "We're college students studying the architecture of old buildings."

The man peered at them suspiciously. "You with that group I saw in here yesterday?"

The Hardys and Larry looked at each other. "Group?" Frank said excitedly. "Can you tell me how many people there were?"

The man shook his head. "Don't remember. All I know is that they headed up those stairs over there." He pointed to a metal staircase a few feet away.

"You boys got any spare change?" the man asked, pulling a crust of bread from his pocket and chewing on it. "I could sure use a bite to eat."

Frank and Joe and Larry dug into their pockets and came up with a few dollars. The man quickly tucked them away.

"Thanks, fellas," he said. Then he turned and walked away, disappearing into the maze of metal piping.

"Poor guy," Joe said. "I wish we could do more to help him."

Larry shook his head slowly. "I never thought much about guys like that before. Maybe I am selfish and spoiled. I'm going after him. Maybe there's something more I can do. I'll be back in a minute." Before Frank and Joe could stop him, Larry ran after the man.

"Come on," Frank said to his brother. "He'll catch up with us later. We have to find Dad!"

The Hardys approached the staircase and climbed up to the second floor. When they got there, they saw a series of storage rooms.

Frank and Joe suddenly heard sounds coming from a room on their right. They crept toward the room. The door was wide open. Frank stationed himself on one side of the door, Joe on the other. Cautiously, they peered inside.

Two men were sitting at a table. One of the men had a dark beard. The other was Nick Marino. Frank and Joe couldn't see if Fenton and the witness were in the room.

"Look, Vince, I know what cards you've got," Marino was saying irritably. "So don't ask me for a queen if you don't need it!"

Frank and Joe stifled a laugh.

"They're playing Go Fish!" Frank whispered to his brother.

"What a dumb game!" the other man complained. "Why can't we play a *real* card game?"

"This *is* a real card game," snapped Marino. "The boss likes it, and so do I, so can the complaints, Vince."

"Just because Brannigan gave you that crummy old deck of cards to play with when you saw him at the museum yesterday," muttered Vince.

"They're not old, they're antique," Marino

said, standing up. He stuck his hand into an empty bag. "Where's Anna, anyway? She was supposed to be back here with the food an hour ago!"

Marino headed toward the doorway. The brothers held their breaths and pushed their backs against the wall. They hoped Marino wouldn't spot them in the dim light.

"Better check our guests again," Marino said, leaving the room. He walked past the Hardys without noticing them and disappeared into a room across the floor.

Frank pointed to Vince. "Let's go," he whispered. Joe nodded.

The brothers burst into the room, swerving around the table. Joe came in low, tackling Vince before he could even get out of his chair. He pinned the crook's arms as Frank snapped a karate blow to Vince's neck. That took the fight out of Vince. He slumped in the chair, unconscious. "One down," Frank muttered, turning toward the door.

Nick Marino came back into the room with half a bag of cookies.

He took one look at the scene before him and lunged at Frank. Marino's charge sent Frank backward to the floor. Marino knelt over Frank, grabbing him around the throat. Frank frantically tried to break Marino's grip, but he couldn't pull free of those choking fingers.

Joe darted forward but froze as Marino glared at him. "Don't come any closer," the crook growled.

Suddenly Marino groaned and went limp. He let go of Frank and rolled onto the floor, where he lay without moving. Frank looked up and saw Larry Crawford standing over him, rubbing the knuckles on his right hand.

"How's that for timing?" Larry said with a grin. "That punch I gave him should keep him out of commission for a while."

Frank got to his feet quickly. "Come on," he said. "We have to check out that other room."

They hurried to the room Marino had entered. In the corner of the room Frank and Joe found two men, both of whom were bound and gagged. They were slumped in the chairs, their eyes closed.

"Dad!" cried Joe.

Joe and Frank rushed to their father. Joe took the gag out of his mouth and untied him. Larry did the same for the witness.

"He's breathing evenly, and his color is good," Frank said with relief.

"I spotted a chloroform bottle in the other room," Frank said. "They must have put Dad and the witness to sleep so they would be easier to handle."

Fenton began to stir. He opened his eyes and blinked, as if he couldn't believe what he was seeing.

"Joe! Frank!" he exclaimed. "Are you all right?"

"We're fine, Dad," Joe said, helping his father up.

"How are *you?*" Frank asked as he helped Joe with their father.

Fenton moved his head back and forth and rubbed his wrists. "Okay, I guess. Just a little groggy." He looked at the witness tied in the chair, his head on his chest. "How's *he?*"

"He should be coming around soon." Frank said.

He smiled up at his sons and Larry. "But how did you three find us?"

"Remember that old Monopoly game you and Mom gave us for Christmas when we were kids?" Joe asked. "That's how we found you!"

"Huh?" Fenton asked, puzzled.

"I think I can explain," a voice said weakly. They turned and saw that the witness was awake.

"My name is Bernard Thurston," he said. Then he smiled at Fenton. "I take it that you are Fenton Hardy, and that two or more of these young men are your sons."

Fenton introduced himself, his sons, and Larry Crawford. He explained who the captive was and why they were trying to rescue him.

"I'll never be able to thank you all enough," Thurston said. He was in his mid-thirties, tall and frail, with large black-rimmed glasses.

"But about the Monopoly game—I needed something to leave as a clue, when Brannigan's men moved us from some old house where we were being held prisoner. I found a Get Out of Jail Free card from a Monopoly game. . . ."

"You were in Evans's Antique Toy Museum," Joe said. "Frank found the card on the floor."

"So that's where we were," Thurston said. "I hoped someone would find the card. My captors often played Monopoly to pass the time. Brannigan even came by for a game." He rubbed his wrists where his hands had been tied. "What a sore loser!"

"Brannigan is into games," Joe said.

Thurston smiled at Joe. "He's 'into' them more than you know."

Frank was still puzzled. "But I still don't see what the Get Out of Jail Free card meant, as a clue. I couldn't figure out where it was supposed to lead us."

"It wasn't meant to lead you anywhere," Thurston explained. "It was supposed to explain *why* I was taken prisoner, not where I was taken to."

They all listened intently as Bernard Thurston began to explain.

"My father is Kyle Thurston, owner of Consolidated Toys and Games," Thurston continued. "I'm the company's treasurer.

"I called the D.A. to testify that Jack Brannigan was attempting an illegal takeover of my father's company," Thurston said. "He's been doing the same to other companies, in an effort to control the toy and game industry in the U.S. Brannigan stood to make millions if the plan succeeded."

"Brannigan was trying to build a *real* monopoly!" Frank said.

"Right!" Thurston rubbed his neck, getting the kinks out. "He's been buying stocks in the companies at unfair prices by threatening the owners. I was ready to blow the whistle on him. Then they started threatening my younger brothers and sisters. Father was concerned for their safety. He agreed to anything Brannigan demanded."

"But the ledger would provide the evidence you had against Brannigan," Joe said, wiping some dust off Thurston's coat.

"That's what I wanted people to think," Thurston said. "I *do* have the entire business transaction with Brannigan and his lawyer down in my ledger. But that wasn't the way I expected to land someone like Brannigan in jail."

"A decoy," Frank said. "I wondered what kind of bookkeeping entries could prove an illegal takeover. Besides, the ledger could be stolen. You had to have some *hard* evidence."

"Another witness!" Joe guessed. "Someone who heard Brannigan threaten your father!"

Thurston smiled at the Joe. "You two work

well together. I *do* have hard evidence. I was worried it would be stolen if I told anyone, even the police and the D.A. So I let them think I could put Brannigan behind bars with my ledger. Then it *was* stolen, and I was kidnapped. Although with the ledger gone, I'm not sure *why* I was kidnapped."

"Your testimony could have resulted in a widening of the investigation," Fenton pointed out quietly. "Not to mention that a certain private investigator spread rumors that there was a second missing ledger."

"How did you do that, Dad?" asked Frank.

"After the pistol range .demonstration. When Sergeant O'Connor was close enough to the commissioner and me, I started to talk about the missing ledger. Sergeant O'Connor conveniently 'overheard' our conversation. I started suspecting O'Connor when I heard you had spotted him with Fielding at the ballpark. The icing on the cake was his hook-up with Marino after the game.

"My mistake was that I underestimated how quickly Brannigan would strike. They snatched me before we had time to set the trap," Fenton told them.

"But the *real* evidence is in a safe place," Joe said.

"In the company vault," Thurston said. "It's a videotape recording of Brannigan's threats to my father, as well as his plan to buy the company at a very unfair price. I rigged a hidden camera in my father's office when Brannigan and Marcus Delaney came to threaten him. I knew their reputation."

"It was brave of you to stand up to a man like Brannigan," Fenton said.

"Someone had to stop Brannigan," Thurston said. "But first, I took precautions. I got Dad to send my brothers and sisters somewhere safe."

Fenton smiled at Thurston. "Well, I think Jack Brannigan's career is over." Then he looked at his sons. "Now, if you don't mind, would you tell me how you managed to find us?"

"We found another Monopoly card, at the warehouse in Philadelphia." Frank told him.

"So you heard one of the kidnappers say you were being moved from the river warehouse to the water works in Atlantic City," Larry said.

"I couldn't believe my luck!" Thurston said. "When Mr. Hardy and I were alone in the warehouse for a few minutes, I managed to shuffle through the Monopoly cards. My hands were tied behind my back, so he told me when I'd found the Water Works card. When we were dragged out of the building during the fire, I dropped it on the floor."

"We'd better call the police and Commissioner Crawford," Fenton said. "The local cops can pick up Nick Marino, Vince, and the woman."

"I'll call from the van," Frank said. He ran out of the building to the van and called the commissioner. Twenty minutes later, the police arrived. They arrested Marino, Vince, and the woman when she arrived with a bag of hamburgers. Minutes later, Commissioner Crawford arrived in a police chopper with his special undercover investigation team.

"I've been in contact with the local law enforcement agency, and they've just issued a warrant for Brannigan's and Delaney's arrest," Crawford said after hugging his grandson Larry. "They're both missing, but we'll find them. We think they're trying to leave the city."

"He's on a videotape I have, too," Thurston assured him. "Transactions with him are also noted in the ledger."

The Commissioner frowned. "We haven't been able to find your ledger."

Thurston grinned. "That's okay. The information in the ledger is also stored on my office computer. You can use that as evidence against Brannigan and Delaney."

"You seem to have covered your bases quite well," Commissioner Crawford told Thurston. "As soon as Brannigan is brought into custody, you and your family will have nothing further to fear from his gang."

"Well, I think it's time for us to be heading back to Philadelphia." Fenton glanced at his watch, then turned to Frank and Joe. "I'll be flying back in the helicopter while you return in the van. We'll hook up later in the afternoon."

With that the Hardy Boys gave the thumbs-up sign to Larry, after which they walked off to the van.

"I've got a question for you," said Joe during the drive back to Philadelphia. "Where are Brannigan and Delaney?" He looked at his brother. "You know, I've got a strange feeling that until they're both in custody, we're still in danger!"

14 Stakeout

At the Police Administration Building, Frank and Joe sat with their father in Commissioner Crawford's office. The commissioner had given them permission to sit in on his questioning of Sergeant O'Connor and Dennis Fielding.

After Dennis Fielding had told his story, the commissioner looked at Sergeant O'Connor. "Well, sergeant? Why did you help Brannigan set up Larry?"

O'Connor looked around unhappily. The game was over, and he knew it.

"Brannigan and I go way back. Ever since I was a rookie cop. It started out when I busted one of his bookie joints. Then he started paying me to look the other way."

"So you went bad from the start," the commissioner said.

"Yeah," O'Connor said. "I'm not going to lie

136

to you now. It started out with just turning my back on things, but before I knew it, I was in deeper than I wanted to be. I transferred to the police academy to try and get away from him. But he was right after me. And I was in too deep. He had too much on me for me to break away from him."

O'Connor leaned back in his chair and looked at the ceiling.

"And when he found you," Frank said, "he wanted you to make things tough for Larry. You were supposed to make him look bad and get him expelled from the academy. That would make the commissioner and the academy and the Police Department look bad."

"Did you write the warning note and the kidnap note?" Joe asked.

"Marino made me do it. He didn't know you were Fenton Hardy's sons. At first he figured you were part of the commissioner's undercover investigation team. After you showed up at the toy store, he told me to leave the note in your brother's locker. We figured you'd quit the academy when your covers were blown. He got me to write the kidnap note, too."

"Did you steal the pistols and ammo and put them in Larry's locker?" Frank asked.

"I did," admitted O'Connor.

"And did you take a shot at Dad?" asked Joe. The memory of the pistol range demonstration incident made Joe's blood boil.

O'Connor looked nervously at Joe. "It was only a scare tactic. I wasn't trying to shoot him. In case you don't know it, I'm an expert marksman. It's one of the classes I instruct. I knew I could get off a shot or two under cover of the noise of all the other shooting. No one but your father was supposed to know I'd taken a shot at him. He was close enough to where the bullet hit to know he had been shot at.

"No one was supposed to hear the second shot; that was a mistake. When they did, Delaney decided to turn it to his advantage. Make it look like the police academy and the commissioner were incompetent."

"Was Redpath in on the plan?" Fenton demanded.

"No. I tried to get Redpath to expel Larry Crawford. But he isn't working with us. That guy is tough but honest. He didn't know anything. Don't blame him." O'Connor looked up at Crawford. "Redpath wasn't helping me make things tough for Larry. I worked on my own at the academy."

"I'm glad to hear you clear Lieutenant Redpath," Crawford said. "He's a good man and an excellent instructor."

"You kept fanning the jealousy Fielding had for Larry," Frank suddenly said to O'Connor. "You put them together and always left them alone, so Fielding could make Larry look bad. You told Fielding he could do almost anything

138

he wanted. You knew Larry might drown, but you didn't care."

O'Connor looked at him and grimaced. "I guess I didn't care about a lot of things, or anyone. I just cared about myself."

Commissioner Crawford looked sternly at O'Connor and Fielding. "You both played into a criminal's hands by going along with his threats. You didn't do what a conscientious citizen should do, much less law enforcement officers. It's too bad that a citizen like Bernard Thurston, with his family in jeopardy, had to show a sergeant of police and a cadet in training how to deal with such a situation!

"Sergeant O'Connor, I'm going to recommend that you be charged with obstruction of justice to begin with, and kicked off the force. Fielding, you will be expelled from the academy. I can't have either of you as police officers in my department. You both may go to jail because of this, but that's up to a judge to decide."

O'Connor and Fielding looked down at the floor as they were led away by two police officers.

After Fielding and O'Connor had left, the commissioner called on his intercom for a guard to bring Marino into his office.

Marino stumbled into the room, his hands cuffed behind him, resisting an officer who kept a strong grip on one of his arms.

"You were the guy who tampered with our father's car," Frank said.

A smile broke out on Marino's face. "What car?" he asked defiantly.

"And you jumped me outside our motel," Joe said.

"And tried to run us off the Schuylkill River Bridge," Frank added.

"Prove it!" Marino sneered.

"Who's the woman who was working with you?" asked Fenton.

"What woman?" Marino shrugged his shoulders.

"That's a nice act you've got there," Crawford said, staring coldly at Marino. "But let me remind you, you were caught with two kidnapping victims—and your partner says that you were the brains of the kidnap plot. Things might go a little easier for you if you cooperate."

Marino's eyes flickered at Crawford's hard-nosed approach. He thought for a moment, then shrugged. "Yeah, I messed up the car. Yeah, I beaned the kid—just a friendly warning to keep out of my way. Maybe I should've hit him harder!"

"Nice guy," mumbled Joe. "Mind talking about the woman?"

"Her name's Anna Weiss." Marino spat out the words.

"How does she figure in this?" Frank asked.

140

"Brannigan needed a front for his illegal business deals," Marino explained. "He offered her a lot of money, and she jumped at it."

"She has a long record," Commissioner Crawford broke in. "Her store has been used as a front for shady deals before. Delaney must have known that and suggested to Brannigan that they get Weiss to cooperate with them. She'll be charged with kidnapping, too, among other things."

"Just one final question," said Frank. "Where are Brannigan and Delaney now?"

A twisted smile spread across Marino's face. "That's something you'll never find out from me," he said slowly.

The brothers and Crawford pressed the issue, but Marino wouldn't talk. Finally, Crawford told the police officer to take him away.

Larry looked at his grandfather after Nick Marino had gone.

"I suppose *I* might as well make a confession," he said.

His grandfather looked at Larry with a puzzled expression. "The Hardys have cleared you of any wrongdoing at the academy," he said.

"I know, and I'm really grateful." Larry smiled at Frank and Joe. Then he took a deep breath.

"I've decided to drop out of the academy," he said. "It's time for me to make a decision that has been tearing me apart for a long time now. I never wanted to be a policeman. I only enrolled as a cadet for the family's sake. For your sake, Grandfather. I hope it doesn't disappoint you too much."

"But Larry, your father and I always hoped that you'd carry on the family tradition." The commissioner's composure seemed shaken by his grandson's decision. "And wear the shield of honor—"

"I'm proud that my father wore a badge and that you wear one," Larry broke in. "But for a long time now, I've thought about becoming a lawyer instead of a cop. I can still fight criminals. But with a law book instead of a badge."

The commissioner looked at Larry for a long time. Then he nodded.

"It's okay, Larry," the commissioner said, putting a hand on his grandson's shoulder. "I think I've been expecting you to make this decision. Whether you're a lawyer or a cop, I know I'll be proud of you."

"Thanks for understanding," Larry told him. He turned to Frank and Joe. "And thanks for all your help, guys. You're good friends and great detectives!" He smiled and gave them a good-natured salute before leaving the office.

A moment later, the phone rang. Commissioner Crawford picked it up on his desk and listened, then frowned.

"Well, keep looking." He hung up the phone and looked at Fenton and the brothers. "Still nothing on Brannigan's or Delaney's whereabouts. A stakeout has been set up at the airport. Brannigan and Delaney will probably try to skip town."

"Andrew, I'm still part of this case," Fenton said. "I'd like to join the stakeout."

"That's all right with me," Crawford said.

"Got room for two more?" Frank asked.

Fenton gave his approval, and the four of them left for the airport. Frank and Joe took the van; Fenton and the commissioner rode in Fenton's car.

At the airport, the police had found no trace of Brannigan or Delaney. The Hardys and the commissioner waited with the police officers for an hour, but neither Brannigan nor Delaney appeared.

Fenton looked at his sons. "I think it's time we let the police handle the case," he said. "We've done our jobs. Now we should let the police do theirs."

He spoke to the commissioner in private, then they shook hands. The commissioner looked at Frank and Joe.

"I'll never be able to thank you both enough," the commissioner said as he shook each brother's hand. "But your father's right. It's time for the police to take over."

The brothers followed Fenton reluctantly to the airport parking lot to get their van and his car.

A woman in high heels got out of a car and began walking their way. She had bright yellow hair and wore a hat with netting that covered her face. Frank thought she looked too old for the yellow hair and figured it must be dyed, or a wig. Her walk, he also noted, was oddly fast and powerful. An alarm in the back of his head started to ring.

Frank nudged Joe. "There's something strange about that woman," he whispered.

Joe looked at the woman. "Well, she's tall and muscular, but so are a lot of women," he said. But he started walking after her. The woman glanced back and started walking faster.

Suddenly, she turned her ankle and stumbled. Before she could regain her balance Joe tackled her.

Frank and Fenton were amazed as Joe knocked the woman down. Her luggage flew out of her hands as she fell to the ground.

"Joe!" Fenton called out, mystified. "What are you doing?"

Fenton and Frank ran over to Joe.

Joe grabbed the woman by the back of her dress and yanked off her veil and her wig.

Fenton called to the police officers standing nearby. One of them took a look at the woman and let out a low whistle. "Well, what do you know," he said. "It's Marcus Delaney." They handcuffed Delaney and led him away; he was still having trouble walking in his high heels.

Then Frank looked at his brother and said, "One down, one to go."

15 Search and Seizure

"I'll stay here with the commissioner," Fenton told his sons. "You two drive back to the motel and check out."

"But Brannigan might show up at the airport," protested Joe.

"I doubt it," said Frank. "Delaney and Brannigan would never risk trying to leave from the same place."

"I guess you're right," Joe said with a sigh. "We might as well give up and go home."

They climbed into the van and drove away from the airport. But instead of taking the turnoff for the road to their motel, Frank continued toward downtown Philadelphia.

"Where are we going?" Joe asked, puzzled. "This isn't the way to the motel."

Frank nodded. "I know. But it's the way to Jack Brannigan," he said.

"What?"

Frank looked at his brother. "Remember when we were in Atlantic City, standing outside the room listening to Marino and Vince?"

Joe thought for a moment. He pounded the dashboard with his hand. "Vince said something about Brannigan giving Marino a deck of cards—at the museum!"

"Right!" Frank said. "I bet that's where Brannigan's hiding until he feels it's safe enough to get out of the city."

"But wouldn't the police think of looking for him there?" Joe asked skeptically.

"They already have. That's why I think he went back there. He probably thinks it's safe because they've already searched the museum," said Frank. "The police are concentrating on putting up roadblocks and checking transportation out of Philly. They obviously don't think he's still hiding in town."

"But we do," said Joe.

By the time the Hardys reached the old Victorian building, it was almost closing time. People were leaving the museum.

"Sorry, the building is closing. Come back tomorrow," a guard at the door told the brothers.

"We . . . uh . . . I think I left my ring in the men's room. I took it off just a few minutes ago, to wash my hands. Just before I left the museum. Do you mind if I take a quick look?" Frank

147

asked. The guard looked at his watch. "All right, but hurry."

"We'd better split up," Frank suggested as they saw arrows pointing to different rooms where toys and games were on display.

Frank hurried off in the direction of the exhibit room.

Joe started in another direction, stopped, and walked toward a bored-looking guard.

"Uh, excuse me, sir," he said to the guard. "I'm looking for my boss. He was delivering a carton of antique toy soldiers to the basement. Can you tell me how to get down there?"

The guard pointed toward the back of the museum. "All the way to the end of the hall, first door on the right."

Joe walked down the hall as fast as he could. When he reached the end of the hall, a bell rang. The museum was closed.

Joe looked at his watch. They only had a few minutes before the guards would force them to leave.

Suddenly, Frank appeared behind him. "I think we're on the same wavelength," he said to his brother.

"How did you find me?" asked Joe.

"Easy. I just asked a guard if he'd seen a guy with short blond hair."

"Where's the basement?" asked Frank.

Joe pointed to the basement door. "Follow me," he said, as he dashed through the door.

Frank followed Joe through the door, almost falling headlong down a dark, steep flight of stairs.

When they had regained their balance, Frank said, "Maybe *you* should follow *me!*" The Hardys continued carefully down to the basement.

"Let's try the room where I saw the Monopoly game," whispered Frank.

They inched their way across the basement floor, feeling their way carefully in the darkness.

When they got to the room, Joe opened the door. Sitting inside the dimly lit room, his back to them, was Jack Brannigan. He was sitting at a card table puffing on a cigar and playing solitaire.

He got up and slowly turned to face them. His huge bulk seemed to fill the room. He smiled at the brothers, but his eyes were filled with menace.

"I hate guns," he said, flicking his cigar at Frank. "They got no style, you know what I mean? But there's all kinds of games and sport stuff in here." He grabbed something from a shelf—a large sword with an ornate basket hilt. "Now this is a German dueling saber. Real classy. It's how all the German officers in the war movies got those neat scars on their faces." He slashed through the air with his yard of steel. Joe backed away.

Frank reached down and picked up the lit cigar. He held it over his head, directly beneath the sprinkler system. An alarm went off, and water rained down on them.

Two guards, who had heard the alarm, rushed into the basement from the other room. Each had a flashlight and a hand on his gun. They aimed their lights on Brannigan, who was running toward the staircase.

When Brannigan saw them, he froze in his tracks.

"What's going on here?" one of the guards demanded.

"This man is Jack Brannigan. He's wanted by the police!" Frank shouted.

"Jack Brannigan?" said one of the guards. The guard pulled his gun from his holster. "Drop the sword, Brannigan!" He approached the crime boss and took him by the arm. "Come on, Brannigan," the guard said. The two guards led Brannigan toward the stairs.

Joe gave Frank a silent signal. Frank looked puzzled but acknowledged Joe. Frank rushed up behind one of the guards and delivered a karate chop on the back of his neck. At the same time, Joe landed a judo kick behind the knee of the other guard and pulled him from behind.

Both men let go of Brannigan and fell to the floor.

"Brannigan's getting away!" Frank yelled.

Before the guards could get back on their feet, the Hardys raced up the stairs in pursuit of the fleeing crook.

Brannigan scrambled wildly down a hallway, in the direction of a side door.

He grabbed the doorknob and turned it, but the door was locked. Panicking and sweating, he kicked at the handle. The door wouldn't budge.

Joe thought that Brannigan looked like a cornered rat. A big one. He and Frank rushed over to him and pinned his arms behind his back.

"Why aren't those two fake guards after us?" Joe asked his brother.

"They probably split. When they realized we'd get their boss," Frank added, looking at Brannigan.

"How'd you smart kids know they weren't real guards?" Brannigan asked.

Frank looked at his brother. "What tipped you off, Joe?"

"They weren't the same guards I'd seen upstairs. And, they came in from the other room. Plus, neither guard frisked Brannigan. I thought they were too easy on him."

The brothers hustled Brannigan to the lobby of the museum. They found two Philadelphia police officers, who had responded to a call

151

from the night watchman about a disturbance in the museum basement, and several firemen running into the building.

Frank quickly explained to the police officers and the firemen what had happened. The police arrested Brannigan as the firemen shut off the basement sprinkler system.

"This is great!" one of the officers told the Hardys. "We're just out of cadet training. This is our first big arrest. Thanks, guys!"

"You ought to join the police academy and become cadets," the other officer told them. "You'd both make good cops."

Frank and Joe looked at each other and laughed. Then they left the museum behind the two officers and watched as they put Brannigan into their squad car.

"Come on," said Frank. "Let's go back to the van. We can dry off and call Dad. We'll tell him we nabbed Brannigan, then we'll check out of the motel and head home to Bayport."

"I'm proud of you both!" Fenton said after Frank had given him all the details about capturing Brannigan. "And I know the commissioner will be, too."

After Frank had finished talking to Fenton, he and Joe headed back to their motel.

They checked out of their room. As they carried their bags to the van, Joe suddenly stopped.

"What's wrong?" asked Frank.

"That van really needs a wash," Joe replied, shaking his head.

"So, we'll stop at a car wash on the way home," Frank said, getting into the driver's side of the van and throwing his bag in the back.

Joe settled down in the passenger seat and looked at his brother. "You haven't forgotten about our bet, have you? Whoever scored lower in cadet training has to wash and wax the van until the end of the year. Well, it so happens Lieutenant Redpath told me that you scored lower on that quiz than I did. So you lose the bet!"

Frank didn't say anything.

"Unless you want to make a *new* bet," Joe said. "I bet you that I can beat you in a game of Monopoly in twenty minutes."

"Twenty minutes!" exclaimed Frank. "No way!"

"Is it a bet?" asked Joe slyly.

Frank grinned at his brother. "It's a bet," he said, as he started up the engine and they headed home to Bayport.